DEFYING KILAN

HISSA WARRIOR
BOOK 4

DISCLAIMER

This is a work of fiction. Names, characters, businesses, places, events and incidents are either the products of the author's imagination or used in a fictitious manner. Any resemblance to actual persons, living or dead, or actual events is purely coincidental.

All rights reserved:

No part of this book may be reproduced or transmitted in any form or by any means, electronic or mechanical, including photocopying, recording, or by any information storage and retrieval system, without prior permission in writing from the author.

Translation:

Don't steal the stories I worked so hard on, and occasionally cried over. Don't get upset at the absolutely made-up story lines: this is a romance, so of course it isn't realistic, duh! Don't be petty and hate on it because it isn't your kink. We've all got different tastes and there's no shame in that.

Copyright: RK Munin, 2022
Cover Illustration: Natasha Snow Designs
Profession Editing: Jenny Sliger, Owl Eyes Edits and Proofs
ISBN-13: 978-1-962699-08-2

Warning: Author is dyslexic as hell.

The editing and beta reading team: Mary Alegre, Gary Anderson, Martha Collins, and Lauren Meghoo

Feel free to contact me with questions, requests, or comments:
Author@RK-Munin.com

Want to get some free novellas or find links to my social media? Everything's on my website:
www.RK-Munin.com

And, as with many writers, your reviews on Amazon, Goodreads, and/or Kindle help immeasurably, even if it's just clicking on the stars.

Thank you to all my readers!

DEDICATION

Thank you to all my friends who've put up with my introverted and anxious ways for all these years!

CHAPTER

1

Pre-dawn light is just starting to turn night into day as Deena pushes the small glider into the launcher. The glider isn't heavy, and she's certainly strong enough, but it's awkward to push into a launcher by herself. It takes her much longer than she likes to finally get it loaded. Dawn is breaking by the time the glider is ready and she can climb in. With a quick look around to confirm she's still by herself on the small training field full of gilders and practice shuttles, she clambers into the bright scarlet gilder and secures herself in the pilot seat.

She does her pre-check quickly, which is easy since there's very little to check in a machine with no electronics and only the most basic controls. At first, Deena resisted practicing in the gliders. She felt as if it was beneath her skill level to fly equipment that not only couldn't break the atmosphere, but also didn't even have an engine. That all changed after her first flight. It turns out that gilders are just as addicting as flying a powered craft.

With a last look around the field, she presses the control switch to light up the warning beacons, telling anyone standing around that a glider's about to launch. Then she waits for a beat, and with a big grin hits the launch button.

In the millisecond between the button depressing and the glider launching with enough force to push her hard against the seat, she sees Kilan emerge from around one of the buildings surrounding the training field. As usual, he's scowling, and she has just enough time to register him shouting at her, and then she's soaring.

Blue sky above, lush dark green jungle below, and silence except for the air passing against the skin of the glider. She's flown many different types of craft over the years but never felt as at peace as she does in these gliders. If the training center didn't allow access to all pilots and trainees, she'd be tempted to buy a glider for herself. The sensation of quiet flight makes her more joyful than she's felt in a long time.

She knows when she lands there'll be hell to pay. She's not supposed to be in the glider by herself yet, but she couldn't care less. When the Hissa agreed to let her fly their shuttles, they insisted she go through their training course, even though she owned and piloted her own space craft for years. So, here she is, spending every day side by side with Hissa men training to pilot shuttles, gunships, and transports, all the while finding any excuse to get herself some glider time.

Her fellow students are nice enough, if a little obvious, about trying to garner her attention. But one of the flight instructors makes everything unpleasant. Kilan seems to have made it his mission to make her time at the school difficult. She doesn't mind the complicated questions he asks. She hasn't answered one wrong yet. But the way he treats her rankles. He never acknowledges her experience in the field. Never lets her share the expertise that comes from countless hours spent flying all kinds of equipment in every situation imaginable.

He treats her like all the other trainees, and that bothers her to no end. As if she's never flown past the Hissa moons. When she pushes past his reticence and tries to share her experiences with the class, he mocks her.

But her days having to put up with him are numbered. She just needs to keep reminding herself of that fact.

Pointing the glider toward the mountains, she searches out updrafts to carry her even higher. She's going to need a lot of altitude for the next maneuver. It takes time and patience to get the glider to the elevation she wants, but it's worth it when she sees a vast jungle stretching out in all directions. Now she's even above the mountain range, which honestly isn't that tall. The planet of Hissa doesn't have much in the way of topological variation. Most of it is flat land or gently rolling hills covered in thick, dense greenery. The mountain range she's using to find updrafts is one of only two on the whole planet.

If she wanted to, she could probably crest the tallest peak, but that's not what she's after. Banking the gilder, she points the nose down and lets the light craft gather speed into a dive, heading straight for one of the only bodies of open water on the entire planet. Pulling up at the last minute, she skims the top of the water, the glider moving so fast the crystal water below is nothing but a blur. Using the remaining momentum to carry her back up, she's able to get just high enough to clear the trees surrounding the lake.

One treetop might have brushed the belly of her glider. But only brushed.

The lake is located high in the mountains, and once she clears the trees, she can see the training field in the distance. There are no clocks in the glider, so she doesn't know how long she's been flying but decides she better head back. She's missed several classes already. The morning classes she skipped to take this flight aren't mandatory. As long as she passes the knowledge tests, there's nothing Kilan can do to her. But that won't stop him from looking for any excuse to kick her out of the training program.

Unlike every other Hissa, Kilan doesn't like her. She can't blame him. Her personality can be caustic sometimes. But she doesn't understand why he's so interested in her failure. Wouldn't it be better for him if she graduated? Then he would never have to deal with her again!

Setting aside thoughts of Kilan, Deena circles the section of the field set aside for the gliders. There's a small crowd gathered on the end of the landing field. It must be the mid-morning break from the classroom. Deciding to show off a bit, she points her noise into a nice breeze coming off the mountain and feels out how strong the headwind is. Once she has a handle on it, she angles her nose down.

Carefully controlling the descent, she lets her mind flow into the zone where she and the aircraft merge. She doesn't have to think about what she's doing. She feels the input from the controls and instruments and reacts. Her mind is quiet. No thoughts swirling around in her brain. No excess emotions or worries pinging around. It's just her, the wind, and the glider.

As the ground gets closer, she slows the glider's speed, carefully controlling for a stall that would drop her out of the air too soon. Her timing is perfect, and by feathering the controls, she manages to make the gilder appear as if it's hovering in midair, only inches from the ground for a breathless moment. After a second of almost perfect stillness, the glider gently descends as if being lowered by a giant invisible hand. The landing gear touches the ground with barely a bump of impact. Her landing is so perfectly timed that the little plane doesn't even need to roll forward at all, just rests where she set it on the meticulously maintained green field.

There's no engine noise on the field to muffle the shouts of admiration from the Hissa men who gathered to watch her land, and she gives them all a big smile as she starts to unbuckle herself and climb out of the glider.

Suddenly, Kilan is there, pulling the glider open and roughly hauling her out of the light craft, careful to keep his claws sheathed so he doesn't accidentally hurt her. He doesn't let go once she's free of the cockpit, and Deena gasps as he throws her over his shoulder and jumps down from the plane. At least he deposits her on her feet next to the glider instead of carrying her off to ream her out in private.

Just like all other Hissa, this man is tall compared to her, probably just under seven feet. But the difference between him and a human male doesn't stop there. Hissa skin is a uniform light green color, except for the top of their bald heads. Starting just above their eyes, Hissa have a scale pattern that begins at a point and steadily expands until it covers the top and back of their heads. It continues down, following their spines until it fades out at their lower backs. The scale pattern is normally a dark blue but can change with emotions. Shock, pain, or fear can blanch it to a light blue or white. Frustration turns it to a muddy brown, and rage turns it black. She's seen a few Hissa males turn brown before but never white or black. Purple, the color of desire, she sees all the damn time. Just about every male that looks at her flushes purple, at least at first. Some never stop showing purple when they're around her.

Expect for Kilan. His scale pattern never changes color. He either doesn't feel emotions very deeply or has incredible control over his body's reactions.

But she's never been particularly entranced by the color-changing scale pattern. What fascinates Deena about Hissa features is their eyes. All Hissa have hourglass-shaped pupils surrounded by a purple so bright their eyes appear to glow on their own. Kilan's eyes are a lighter shade than most, and she's found herself staring into his eyes a few times, her mind lost in thought, only to be brought back when he asks her a demeaning question or makes a rude comment.

For her, Kilan's the epitome of Hissa beauty. Until he opens his mouth, and then he's the bane of her existence.

Or hauls her out of a glider.

Putting her hands on her hips, she refuses to be intimidated as he stares down at her, his light purple eyes bright with anger. Deena glares right back at the glowering Hissa. "Uncalled for, Kilan."

She keeps her spine straight and her gaze unwavering, even though he towers over her. She might be on the small side for a Decanted female, standing only five-four compared to her friend Lara's five-ten, but she refuses to let anyone intimidate her. Especially not this pompous, conceited, flight instructor. "You didn't need to manhandle me like that."

"You didn't have permission." His voice is close to a roar. For the first time, she sees his scale pattern flash black. But it's so quick she almost missed it. "You know better!"

"I'm on the roster," she points out quickly, taken aback by his rage. Blinking, she watches his blue scale pattern flash to black again for only a brief moment, then back to dark blue. Wow, he must really be pissed. He takes a very deliberate half-step back and visibly reins in his anger.

"You're on the roster to launch now with me as your trainer." He's no longer loud, but his tone is still harsh. "You deliberately came early to avoid flying with me." There's a note of some kind of emotion there. If she didn't know better, she'd think his feelings were hurt. "There's a reason you fly with an instructor. The jungles of Hissa are a dangerous place. Even a male with skill and knowledge can be consumed by them. If you were forced down alone, there's a high probability you wouldn't survive."

Ah, there's the reason for so much emotion: worry. He's probably not personally anxious about her dying in the jungle. He doesn't like her after all. But as the only single, breeding compatible female on the planet for the moment, he probably would have gotten in big trouble if anything happened to her.

She can understand that. It's similar to having

responsibilities over an expensive ship. That makes her annoyance disappear, replaced with a small amount of sympathy. Besides, the morning flight was too wonderful and the landing too perfect to stay in a bad mood, even after being the recipient of Kilan's unnecessary high-handed behavior.

"You don't let me do anything fun when we fly together." She gives him a wide, unrepentant grin. "Besides, nothing happened. I'm back safe and sound. And you've got to admit, that landing was sublime."

It's obvious he's fighting to keep from smiling. "You're very skilled, but we have rules for a reason."

"I'm not the reason," she retorts and points over to the other trainees standing around watching. "They're the reason. I'm only here because the Council's too cautious."

His almost-smile vanishes.

"You will follow the school's curriculum, or you won't fly," he declares grimly. "If you fly one more time without a trainer, I'll personally bar you from this session, and you'll need to wait for the next set of trainees to start all over again." Deena gapes at him for a moment. His gaze doesn't waver, so she knows he's serious.

"Low blow," she mutters and then forces a fake, overly sweet smile on her face. "I won't break the rules again," she promises and turns to stalk off to join a group of nearby Hissa trainees. Her smile becomes genuine as they all greet her enthusiastically.

"That was an amazing landing, Deena."

"How did you make the glider hover like that?"

"After we graduate, will you take me up in the glider and teach me those maneuvers?"

"We saw you dive to the lake, some thought you wouldn't recover, but I knew you're too skilled to crash."

The compliments are interrupted when Kilan marches over and waves everyone to the classroom.

"Move," he orders. "We're behind schedule." With good-natured comments, they ignore Kilan's familiar brusque behavior and make their way into the classroom.

As usual, Deena is pushed to the seat of honor in the front with the men jostling for the spots around her. She ignores them and slumps down in her seat, pushing her legs out in front of her, then crossing them at the ankles. She folds her arms over her chest and pointedly doesn't pull out a data pad to review assigned readings or pull out a sheet of memory paper to take notes.

Eyes narrowed with animosity; she silently watches Kilan make his way to the front of the classroom. Her expression is daring him to comment about the empty desk in front of her.

She never takes notes and only glances at the texts they assign, and yet scores perfectly on every knowledge test and practical exercise. She knows it drives Kilan crazy and that makes all of this almost bearable. The truth is, she spent her teenage years learning to fly and then almost her entire adult life working and living onboard various ships. She's got a wide base of experiences and knowledge to draw on that rivals any of the professional Hissa pilots.

He pointedly ignores her.

"Today we'll discuss different types of engines, their applications, and what to use if your ship comes equipped with both boosters and thrusters."

It's all too rudimentary. Deena barely manages to keep from sighing and reminds herself she's only a week away from graduation. One week and she gets to fly in space again. She'll do just about anything to get back out there. It's been fun to live planet side, but the need to fly is too strong to ignore. She needs off-planet before she goes stir crazy, especially now that Lara is emotionally stable and deeply in love with her mate, Selon. Lara doesn't need her around for hand-holding any longer and that means it's time for Deena to figure out some way to get her ass back in a pilot's seat. For now, her path to space includes putting up with Kilan and this training.

Whatever. She's dealt with worse.

"Let's review the reading assignment," Kilan continues. "What's the proper application for a C-rated engine?" Deena opens her mouth to answer, but Kilan glares down at her. "You aren't to answer today. You only get to talk if you have a question to ask. Do you understand?"

Seething, she gives a sharp nod of her head. She feels mildly better when she notices the other students all glaring at Kilan. The way he singles her out for reprimand at least once a class doesn't go unnoticed.

Not that she doesn't deserve the occasional rebuke. She is a bit of a smart ass. But on the other hand, everyone knows she doesn't belong here. Her skill level could have easily been tested to allow her to fly Hissa ships without needing to send her through the entire training program.

When the Council first told her she needed to train to fly, she fought them. It took her a few days and a lot of arguments before she finally figured out this is the Council's sneaky way of trying to bar her from flying. Or at least delay it.

The Council probably hopes one of the other trainees or trainers will catch her attention, mate her, get her pregnant, and she'll settle down to be a Hissa broodmare.

Wishful thinking.

She must have snorted out loud because Kilan casts her a reproving look. She rolls her eyes at him, and he frowns, then returns to the topic at hand.

Just one more week, she thinks again. *One more week and I get to fly, and I won't need to deal with Kilan anymore. He must be the only Hissa on the entire planet who's not interested in getting in my pants.*

It's not just that he doesn't want to have sex with her. That's fine in her book. It's the fact that he genuinely seems not to like her. She might be a bit obnoxious occasionally, but she's a good person. How she got on his bad side mystifies her. She did steal his chair at a Council meeting to stand on once, but it was just a chair. That shouldn't have caused this level of animosity.

These thoughts depress her a little. She knows she can be hard to deal with sometimes, but all the other males seem to go out of their way to make her feel welcome, although she's a little tired of being pursued. There needs to be a happy medium between Kilan's hostility and constant bombardment for attention from all the other Hissa males.

If she puts her foot down, the Hissa men do back off and give her a little space, but not for long. They're all desperate for mates and children, and right now she's the only unmated female on the whole damn planet.

Which is one of the reasons she needs to get off this jungle-covered rock.

She can't blame the men. If she was in their situation, she's not sure she'd act with as much honor, patience, or kindness as the Hissa do.

Over a decade ago, a deadly plague the Hissa refer to as the Great Death killed every Hissa female and almost half their males, leaving their civilization with a gaping hole, both literally and figuratively. Exhausting every avenue, the Hissa had almost resigned themselves to extinction when Mara, a Decanted human, saved an enslaved Hissa male named Tiran. Things got hot and heavy between the two, and to everyone's surprise, mating marks appeared around Mara's neck, telling the world she's biologically compatible with Tiran. The Hissa scientists soon verified this.

In short, something about the DNA used to create the Decanted humans back in the Earth system makes the females breeding compatible with Hissa males.

That discovery infused the Hissa with hope for the revitalization of their species. In response, the Hissa mobilized. They sent ships out to find every Decanted female sold into slavery and also to retrieve Mara's twin sister, Lara, separated years earlier when they'd been sold from one place to another.

Deena had befriended Lara after the sisters were separated. The two of them had been reasonably successful independent freight haulers until they were attacked by raiders. The Hissa military swooped in just in time to save the two of them. Originally, they focused on rescuing Lara, knowing she's Decanted and could have children with a Hissa male of her choice. When they found out Deena was also Decanted, they saw her as a bonus.

But she's not just Decanted, she's a Special. Specials are Decanted children that are specifically ordered with certain traits that humans don't normally have. Unlike the sisters Mara and Lara, Deena wasn't grown to be sold into slavery. She was bought by a wealthy family to be the wife of a rich man living on a colony far from Earth.

After being grown for six months in a vat, she was Decanted at the biological age of six, the oldest they could grow a child without risking damage. She spent another six months being trained as instructors unpacked all the information implanted in her brain while she was matured in the viscous fluid of an artificially fabricated womb. Once trained, she was shipped off to her new "family."

Absently, she rubs a scar that runs the length of the skin behind her ear and down the back of her neck. The scar is an unmistakable indicator she's Decanted, it's where the implants are put while the children grow in the vats. The implants program the children's brain with language and motor skills so when they are Decanted, they can talk and walk like any other six-year-old, despite the fact that technically, they're actually newborns.

There are generally two reasons Decanted children are ordered. They're either meant to be slaves or children to a family who doesn't have the time or ability to have their own.

Sometimes, it's difficult to figure out the difference

between slavery and childhood.

The Addingtons, the family that purchased her, didn't want a child. Her childhood was just something they had to put up with because the Decanting technology can't create fully grown adults.

The first member of her new family that she met was an elder woman with a stern face and cold eyes. When she tried to hug the woman, she was pushed aside.

"Never do that again," the elder instructed tiny Deena. "We don't touch like that here. You'll maintain your distance, remain quiet unless asked a question, and stay out of everyone's way. You'll call me Mother. Do you understand all this?"

After being programed and trained, Deena might have the body of a six-year-old, but her mind operated at the level of a child of ten with the knowledge base of someone who achieved multiple degrees.

"Yes, Mother," Deena replied dutifully.

"While we wait for you to mature, you will study, stay physically fit, and attend functions with us," Mother explained to her. "Once you reach your menses, you'll marry my son and produce grandchildren for me. That's all that is required of you. In exchange, you won't be beaten or starved. You'll have fine clothes, eat expensive foods, and live in luxury. Now you can thank me for all I'm providing you."

"Thank you, Mother." Even at that tender age, Deena knew this wasn't how things were supposed to be done, but instinctively, she knew not to say anything.

Her life wasn't bad for the next six years. She never received any type of affection from her new family, not even her future husband, Gregor. He rarely even talked to her and often sent her away early from communal meals. But the staff were kind to her, and one of the tutors fought to get her flying lessons. Those were good years, full of exploration and some affection from those hired to care for her.

That all changed the first time she bled between her legs. Mother was pleased, but Gregor looked resigned. The marriage ceremony was quick and without frills. The rest of the marriage is something Deena tries very hard not to think about.

It doesn't matter anymore. I'm free now. The words are easy to think, but the way she is effectively trapped on Hissa makes them feel like lies.

She meets the eyes of the Hissa sitting to her right. He

looks concerned, and she realizes her face must be reflecting her unhappy thoughts. She curves her lips into a derisive smile and then rolls her eyes to Kilan. The male follows her eyes and gives a little frown at the instructor and then looks back to Deena.

His expression changes to sincere interest, and he leans toward her. "I don't understand the importance of atmospheric entry angle," he whispers to her. "Would you be willing to explain it to me later?"

"Do you have a question, Havin?" Kilan draws their attention, his voice full of censure and annoyance. "If you are too shy to ask questions here in class, you can approach any instructor individually. That's what we're here for. Having students teach students is a good way to learn bad habits."

Although Deena's annoyed at Kilan's high-handed behavior, she's relieved she doesn't have to tell Havin no. Most of her fellow trainees accepted her rebuffs good naturedly, but Havin keeps pushing. She's worried she'll have to do something forceful soon and doesn't want to be pushed into that particular corner.

She's stuck on Hissa for now. With no money and no ship, there's no way for her to get off-planet, but she has a plan. Although they don't want her to leave, the Hissa will be forced to start paying her a wage when she pilots for them. It shouldn't take long for her to save up enough money to buy passage to one of the bigger stations, like Wint. She's a damn good pilot and getting a job there will be easy. It's going to be a long haul to save enough for another ship of her own, but that's the end goal. Her own ship and independence.

She can't tell the Hissa any of this. They're indulging her with these classes and the promise of getting to pilot their cargo shuttles only to placate her.

"Good luck with that," she mutters.

"I didn't quite hear what you said, do you have a question?" Kilan is standing right in front of her desk, hands resting on the surface as he stares down at her. Pienter shit, how long was he standing there while she was lost in thought?

"If you have both boosters but lose secondary stage ignition during ascent but you haven't broken the first gravity tier yet, should you try to reignite or abort?" The words roll effortlessly off her tongue. His eyes widen briefly. He wasn't expecting that. Deena smirks at him as he goes silent as he formulates an answer.

Ha! No one's ever ready for Deena, and that's the way she likes it.

CHAPTER 2

One Week Later

"You know, considering you don't like me very much, I'm surprised you always end up as my flight instructor," Deena comments as she follows Kilan to a nearby training shuttle. "I guess it's a little late to say anything because this is our last flight together, but I've got to point this out. You could've handed this duty off to any number of other instructors. You're not even on the testing roster right now. You didn't need to do this, to fly with me for my test."

Her words bring him up short, and she almost runs into his broad back. Kilan swings around to face her, his face a combination of surprise and hurt. "Why would you think I don't like you?"

Taken aback, Deena shrugs. "You're always yelling and scowling at me, even when I'm not making smart remarks. I don't know if I've ever seen you smile. All the other guys smile and laugh with me, but you go out of your way to frown."

"I don't smile at anyone," he grumbles. "You shouldn't take it personally."

Unsure of what to say, Deena falls back on the caustic part of her personality. "Nice to know you're equally mean to everyone. You must be the only Hissa I've met who's never asked me to go home with him or tried to give me something. Don't blame a girl if she takes it personally."

He takes a step closer to her and leans over, looking sincerely interested. "Would you let me take you home or accept a gift from me if I offered?"

Unprepared for his abrupt change in attitude, she finds herself hesitating before answering. "Well, no, of course not."

His face goes blank, and she finds it disconcerting when he leans a little closer to her. She wants to step back but doesn't want to show weakness. What kind of game is he playing?

"You hesitated," he murmurs. "Why did you hesitate and then say, 'of course not?'"

"I don't accept anyone's offer," Deena points out quickly, finding herself unwilling to hurt his feelings for some reason. He's so close she can smell him now. Just like every other time she's caught his scent, she's forced to fight the urge to touch him. To draw his body to her and run her hands all over him. Images of putting her face against his neck and breathing him in are so vivid it makes her momentarily dizzy.

And just like every other time this happened, she ignores her body's demands.

She takes a quick step back, ignoring the look of triumph on his face. She's much too concerned about the effect his smell has on her to bother with his gloating. Her urges feel stronger today than normal, and that worries her.

I must be close to going into heat, she thinks and makes a mental note to see one of the Hissa menders for medication. Nothing stops the heats, but with enough drugs, she can just spend a few days knocked out instead of in pain.

It's true that the Council frowns on her using drugs instead of picking a male, but they aren't refusing her access to medications. And no way is she going to let herself go into heat around all these men!

She does a quick mental calculation and decides she has enough time to complete her flight with Kilan and reach a mender before her heat cycle really sets in.

"You're just trying to distract me from my final test flight," she retorts. Her accusation is just a ploy to throw him off and redirect the conversation, but she must have hit a nerve because Kilan takes a step away from her, his scowl returning.

"I'm not as underhanded as you think," he growls out. "I was only taking a moment to assure you I don't dislike you."

"Great!" Deena shoots back with mock enthusiasm. "Now that's all cleared up, let's get this flight going."

Body stiff, Kilan turns and marches to the waiting practice shuttle, leaving her to follow or not. With a small growl of her own, she trudges after him, thankful she'll never have to deal with him again after today.

This flight is her last test, and once she's successfully completed it, she will be a certified pilot for the Hissa. The only thing she wouldn't be allowed to pilot are military ships during combat.

Just another few hours and I'm done living in houses and walking on the ground. Just another few hours and I can be back in space, doing the only thing I'm good at. It's the same pep talk she's been giving herself for weeks, only the amount of time she has to endure changes. Now that it's down to hours, she finds herself more anxious than ever. She's afraid that if she's forced to stay planet side even another day, she might grow roots into the Hissa soil and sprout leaves.

It doesn't take them long to reach the far end of the field where the practice shuttles are parked. While Kilan opens the hatch, she circles the shuttle, doing a visual inspection of all surfaces, looking for any cracks, pits, or damages that might impair flight. She knows this is the first part of the test, so she takes her time and finishes by tapping a cable that looks slightly worn.

Kilan silently watches her and then steps up to her side when she points out the cable. "We might want to pick another shuttle. Lara should look at this one."

He leans over her to study it and shakes his head. "It's not rusted. That's dirt. It won't cause any issues."

Deena shrugs. "Fine, but if anything goes wrong, it's on the record. I noticed it and reported my findings." She thinks he almost smiles at her words, but instead, he nods his head solemnly. In truth, she agrees with him, but she's navigating this test with an over-abundance of caution.

"Your findings are noted. Let's proceed to the inside pre-flight check."

She leads him inside, and they settle into the side-by-side

seats at the front of the shuttle. Deena runs through the pre-flight check of the shuttle's systems. Kilan doesn't comment, just watches her with a grim expression. If she was any less experienced, she'd find his expression forbidding and intimidating. But because she's Deena, and no frowning, disapproving Hissa is going to keep her from flying, she doesn't miss a beat.

By the time she's done, the engine is rumbling and ready for launch, the navigation computer programed, instruments are all calibrated, and she's cleared by the flight coordinators to launch and burn for Diminish, the smaller of Hissa's two moons. She looks over at him with a raised eyebrow.

"Is pre-flight check completed to your satisfaction, Instructor Kilan?" she gives him a big cheeky grin. If anything, his expression turns a little sour.

"You've performed adequately so far. Proceed to Diminish."

She gives a little nod and turns her attention back to the shuttle's controls. It might only be a milk run to a close moon, but it's flying and she's ecstatic. She wants to wiggle in her seat and laugh as the engine's ramp-up, vibrating the shuttle around them.

As she launches, she feels something off. She can't put her finger on it, but something doesn't feel quite right. This is one of those times she wishes Lara was here. That woman is the finest mechanic she ever worked with and would be able to pinpoint the issue in seconds. But Deena doesn't have Lara with her, just a surly Hissa who'll probably take any comment she makes about the shuttle feeling odd as an opportunity to deduct points from her final score. That means there's no point in saying anything unless an actual error pops up on her control panel.

They're in the air now, pushing high into Hissa airspace. She can feel a shimmy in the controls. Everything's responding to her input, but sluggishly, and she's forced to constantly adjust to compensate for slow response time.

A loud bang at the rear of the shuttle sets off a violent shuddering in the controls. Alarms start to sound from the control console, and Deena fights the shuttle as it tries to nosedive back to the ground.

"The starboard thruster tank is ruptured," Kilan reports as his hands fly over the control console. Deena's surprised he isn't trying to take control of the shuttle away from her, but then again, he's a seasoned pilot also and knows her skill level. They'll both need to have hands on the control console if they're going to survive this.

"I've got severe yaw angle to starboard, and I'm pitching down," she reports. "Estimate three more minutes of flying time."

"Engine is shut down, and fuel neutralizers are deploying," Kilan tells her.

The controls stop fighting her at the same time she loses significant engine thrust. Kilan's fingers fly over the controls. "Routing all port thrusters to fire in line with offline engine."

"That helps," Deena grits out as she's able to use Kilan's reconfigured thrusters to stave off freefall. "But this is going to get bumpy."

The topographical display tells her she's about to land in the middle of the dense jungle, far from Hissa's only major city. These shuttles are tough and should take a lot of damage before either of them gets hurt, but there is no way she can make this landing soft. "Brace yourself."

She uses everything the shuttle has left to pitch up just as they get close to the ground. She manages to keep the yaw angle neutral and aims them into the least crowded bit of jungle she can find. The moment she feels the first impact on the shuttle, she hits the kill switch that shuts down every system in the ship, stopping any additional thrust and potentially helping to slow them down.

The cabin goes dark, and she braces.

The shuttle hits hard and violently quakes around them. A series of bangs and thumps sound as they're thrown around in their seats. When everything stops, Deena scrambles to get herself unbuckled from the seat. The next order of business is to get out of the shuttle before anything else goes wrong with it.

The only thing she can see in the dark shuttle is a few faintly glowing lights, but that doesn't slow her. She spent so much time in this type of shuttle that she could navigate the interior with a bag over her head. She stands up and reaches for Kilan, worried he might not know which way to turn in the dark.

"We've—" Her words end in a squeak when big hands grab her, haul her up against a big hard body, and roughly carry her to the shuttle door. She feels him strain against the door and finally gets it open with a shriek of mental and the sound of breaking servos. Holding onto her tightly, he jumps down just as an ominous creaking sound comes from the ground under the shuttle.

She's folded over his shoulder like a bag of tubers as he sprints from the downed craft. She lifts her head just in time to see their shuttle disappear in a puff of steam.

Stopping at what he must deem a safe distance, he puts her down, and they both stare at the empty air where their ruined shuttle sat just a moment ago.

"What just happened?" she whispers,

"Geothermal," Kilan explains briskly as he grabs a fistful of her shirt and drags her deeper into the jungle. "You landed us right next to one. The weight of the shuttle collapsed the earth under it and made the geothermal hole bigger. By now, it's probably about a mile underground and melting. We need to move further away."

She doesn't struggle in his hold and just waits for Kilan to decide they're a safe distance from the geothermal, which doesn't take long. When he does stop, he doesn't look at her. He's busy examining the area around them.

Deena looks back to where she landed. The path of destruction the shuttle wrought through the jungle is very clear, but she knows Hissa jungle plants grow so fast, it'll disappear in mere minutes.

"Well, any landing you can walk away from, and all that," Deena mumbles and does an internal check for injuries. Just a few bumps and bruises, nothing serious. She doesn't even bother to ask Kilan if he's hurt. Hissa are an incredibly tough species. It would take a lot more than a bumpy landing to do damage to one of them. "So how long until our ride shows up?"

"Ride?" Kilan turns to look at her, his expression sullen. "They won't find us. Did you not hear the part where I mentioned our ship is busy melting?"

"Right, melting," she bites her lip, looking back toward the geothermal vent. "Everything's melting. The ship and the distress beacon that would tell our rescuers exactly where we are in this big Hissa jungle. What percentage of your planet is jungle again?"

"84%," Kilan reminds her grimly. "The path the shuttle made is already disappearing. We're in the middle of the jungle, far from the only city on Hissa. We have no survival gear. And you're a weak human."

"You sure know how to charm a girl," Deena mutters. Kilan ignores her and continues.

"There are small shacks built in a grid pattern throughout the jungle. They're equipped with gear and small comm arrays. We just need to get to one of those."

"That sounds like good news," Deena states cautiously. Kilan's expression turns downright cantankerous.

"If my guess is correct, the nearest shack is a full day's walk for me alone. If I drag you along, it might take up to three days. That means at least one night spent in the jungle, perhaps two."

Deena looks around at the dense greenery surrounding them. Kilan's attitude is starting to get to her. What would be worse, trying to survive in this wild place by herself or putting up with this constantly cranky Hissa?

"I don't want to be the reason you need to spend the night in the wild. You just run ahead, and I'll follow as fast as I can." That makes him growl. "Did you just growl at me?"

"It's a natural reaction to hearing a suggestion that foolish," Kilan retorts, and Deena feels like he slapped her. Engine failure can happen to anyone. They're in a bad situation, sure, but it could be so much worse, including dying in a fiery wreck or melting with the shuttle far down in a geothermal vent. Considering those things, and the fact that they're still alive, she is damn tired of Kilan's attitude.

"I know you won't believe me, but I wasn't put in this universe just to annoy you," she snaps back at him. "Sorry to be so weak and feeble but telling me I'm foolish isn't the most helpful feedback. Now, want to try that again?"

He stares at her in silence, the expression on his face going from annoyance to indecision and finally rests on pensive. "I spoke out of frustration. I apologize."

"Accepted," Deena concedes easily. "Now that's taken care of, let's get back to the whole survival thing."

"That's what has me upset," he admits. "There are no good solutions in this situation. I can't leave you alone in the jungle overnight. And besides that, if I leave, I run the risk of not being able to find you again. That means we need to stay together. Staying together means a night in the jungle. It'll be uncomfortable and potentially dangerous. We don't have many large predators, but we do have quite a few smaller venomous ones. There's no option here where I can get you to one of the shacks or any other place of safety before nightfall."

Now Deena understands why Kilan got so frustrated so fast; he's worried about keeping her comfortable and safe. She feels a small warmth uncurl in her chest at the thought that he cares about her well-being.

Then a cramp hits her midsection, and she doubles over.

"I might have more bad news," she mumbles through the

pain. He's kneeling next to her now, helping her to sit on the ground.

"Did you sustain an internal injury in the crash?"

"No," Deena looks up at him and tries to smile but ends up gritting her teeth instead. "I'm about to go into heat."

The look of horror on his face freezes out any warm feelings she might have been developing for him. The cramp becomes more intense, and she drops her gaze to the ground, concentrating on breathing through it and trying not to panic because she's never gone into heat this quickly.

"Oh, good job me. I'm stranded deep in the jungle with the one Hissa who doesn't want to have sex with me, and I start my heat cycle. I've always had lousy timing," she gripes.

Predictably, Kilan doesn't comment as he gives her a pained look. Then finally says, "I didn't think this situation could get worse."

"What can I say," she sighs out as the cramp starts to ease up, "I'm an overachiever."

DEFYING KILAN 25

CHAPTER 3

None of the other Decanted humans recovered so far go into a heat cycle when they're in estrus. All the other females have normal human reproductive cycles. Except for Deena.

Caustic, arrogant, abrasive Deena, who even now is panting from the pain. Her normally light brown skin is pale and covered in a light sheen of sweat, and he can hear her mumbling to herself. He stands up and puts a little distance between them, so her alluring fragrance isn't so strong.

He needs to pull himself together. This disaster isn't her fault and exposing her to his temper won't help things.

"What can I do to ease the symptoms?" he asks, and she rolls her eyes to look up at him.

"Besides the obvious?" she bites out.

"Obvious?"

"Yeah, obvious!" she shouts at him, her face flushing. "Getting your dick out and fucking me."

Although he's used to her bluntness, her explicit words throw him. The panic must show on his face because she casts him a murderous glare before closing her eyes.

What she doesn't understand is that he wants to bed her in the worst way. He's fought his attraction to her since the first day he met her when she helped Lara defend Selon in front of the Council. He can easily imagine doing many pleasurable things to her.

But he can't risk it. Can't risk letting himself feel again. Never again.

He tries to keep his voice neutral. "I don't want to bed you."

"That, I know," she gripes. "It should have been Galin or Nelom or anyone else on this flight with me. Anyone but you."

He doesn't take offense. She's not wrong. Every other unmated Hissa on the planet would be overjoyed to switch positions with him and service her through her heat. They wouldn't hesitate to fill her with their seed. And they'd also be enraptured when mating marks appeared around her neck. For a brief moment, he pictures her with mating marks around her neck. Mating marks he put there. The marks mean the couple are biologically compatible. The marks mean they can have children together.

He ruthlessly banishes the image. She's not for him. No one is for him.

"Leave it to me to go into heat where I don't have any drugs, and the only male around thinks I'm atrocious," she grumbles. Her words make him feel ashamed.

"I don't think you're atrocious," he argues. Should he explain? Should he tell her about—

"Just shut up," she groans, curling into herself. Now is not the time for talking. That takes one difficult decision off the table.

"Do I need to put my seed inside you, or will an orgasm alone ease your symptoms?"

"Orgasms help," she admits.

"How long does your heat last?" he asks

"Anywhere between two to five days," she explains and starts panting. "Damn, this one came on fast. I've never had one start so fast or hurt this bad."

"Maybe you're reacting to something on Hissa," he suggests and starts looking around for a Narlo plant.

"Who cares why?" she counters between pants. "Get over here and help a girl out or go away because your smell is driving me insane."

That surprises him. He knows the Decanted women have superior senses compared to root stock humans, but he can't imagine why his smell would be bothering her so much. Then it hits him. He's male. The smell of any male nearby would probably set her off while she's in heat.

He hurries to pull the large, soft leaves off a nearby Narlo plant and places them on the ground next to her to form a kind of bed. Once he's done, he encourages her to recline on it and reaches for the closure to her pants.

She catches his hands in hers. "What do you think you're doing?"

"Easing your symptoms?"

She raises an eyebrow at him. "I thought you didn't want me."

"I'm not going to have sex with you," he explains. "I'll use my mouth and my hands to bring you to climax. You said it helps."

"Oh, got it," she says and pulls her hands away from his. He notes she seems almost disappointed in his answer. "Never let it be said you didn't do your duty," she grumbles.

He ignores her words and focuses on stripping her of her boots and pants. The smell of her arousal is thick in his nose, making his mouth water and his cock harden. What would it be like, to just give in this once? Deena isn't some naïve inexperienced female. Surely, she doesn't expect anything more from him than relief from her heat. He could have this time with her, enjoy her, and walk away after. He'd never need to see her again.

For some reason that thought doesn't fill him with the relief it should. Determined to make sure she understands their situation, he draws back a little, fighting the urge to dive between her legs.

"I need you to open your eyes and look at me," he commands.

Panting, Deena focuses on his face. "What's up? Changed your mind? If you want to go off and find one of those shacks, I'll just stay here and keep myself entertained." Her words are meant to be amusing, but the tone is clipped and biting.

"I'm not leaving," he assures her. "But you need to promise not to get attached to me."

She snorts out an inelegant laugh. "Annoying, bad-tempered, surly, and exasperating: what's not to love?"

"I'm not surly or exasperating," he retorts, feeling stung by her words. Does she see him in such an unflattering light? He's a good instructor, and if he's hard on her, it's only because he knows she's far more advanced than any of the other students. Even if he's a little sharp with her, it's due to her own quarrelsome nature.

"If I say you're everything sweetness and light, will you give me some relief?" she bites out.

Her words pull him out of his thoughts and back to the issue at hand, pleasuring the sweet-smelling female before him. He parts her legs and kneels between them. There's no resistance from her, she's closed her eyes again, her arms curled protectively over her belly. Her skin feels damp and hot to the touch.

"Tell me if I hurt you," he murmurs as he lowers himself down. The apex of her legs is right in front of his eyes, commandeering all his attention. The dark curly hair there is soft, and he takes a moment to enjoy the texture of it against his fingers. Hissa don't have any hair on their body, and he's heard many males wonder what the Decanted female's hair feels like, not that he'll tell them it's softer than the finest cloth credits can buy. And their skin is creamy and warm to the touch. Or that they smell so delicious that it can make a male's mind stop working and instinct takes over.

All these thoughts swirl around in his head as he gently parts the lips of her sex with shaking fingers. Before him is pink glistening flesh and the small button of nerves he knows he must pay close attention to. She appears so delicate. Could his big hands hurt her by accident? Or even his tongue? He knows he must be careful of his long canines, but could even the flat of his tongue cause harm?

Lara, Mara, and Mian, the other Decanted women mated to Hissa men, seem to have no problem with their mates. What he wouldn't give to have a quick conversation with any of those males just to get a little insight into pleasuring a Decanted female.

For the first time in his life, he wishes he'd visited one of the traveling brothels that used to visit their planet regularly.

"Are you doing an examination down there?" she asks without opening her eyes. "What's the hold-up? You need to start touching me!"

For the first time in the short history of their interactions, her scathing tone doesn't irk him. Instead, he finds himself smiling at her ability to be bitingly witty despite her pain and discomfort.

"Lucky doctor that gets to see to your health," he murmurs

to her. "Lucky clothing that sits so close to this beautiful body. Lucky me for being in the right place at the right time." He meant his words to be soothing, flattering, and perhaps even help her relax, but instead, she tenses and opens her eyes to send him a sharp look.

"Don't do that," she orders flatly.

Were the compliments too clumsy? He's unpracticed at the art of seduction. And because he doesn't want a mate of his own, he hasn't bothered reading any of the reports issued by the Council about human culture and the Decanted women. Did he just insult her by accident?

"Don't pretend I'm pretty or that you like me. It'll make me feel like a whore," she elaborates, giving Kilan an insight he's not entirely comfortable with. What must it be like to suffer these heats as a free woman and need to find a male or drug yourself to oblivion? He feels like a dim-witted fool. But he won't retract his statements. They're nothing but the truth.

"You're precious," he says as he strokes a finger along her sex. "Just because I don't want a mate, doesn't mean you aren't beautiful and desirable."

She doesn't respond, just sounds a needy little moan as his fingers play around her clit. Her hips move against his hand, and he increases the pressure. It's a relief to know his fingers aren't too rough for her. He rubs her for a few moments until her sounds go from joy to frustration.

"More!" she demands.

He slips two fingers into her and brings his face down to suck her clit into his mouth. Convulsing, she climaxes quickly, and he draws back, mildly disappointed that he got only the briefest taste of her. He withdraws his fingers and gives into his impulses and brings his fingers to his mouth to suck them clean. The taste of her is exquisite.

"Thanks," she mumbles, pulling her legs away from him and curling up on her side. He reaches out to rest a hand on her hip. Her skin is still hot to the touch. Two to three days, he reminds himself. This is only the first taste. There'll be plenty more in the coming days.

He looks around them. There's no water in this section of the jungle. In fact, there's little open and easily accessible water anywhere on Hissa. Although he can go several days without drinking, he knows Deena can't. He needs to get them both to the shack and call for help. If he tries to wait out her heat here, they could both end up perishing.

"Can you walk for a while?" he asks. "Or I can carry you. I'd like to make progress to the closest shack before dark."

"Yeah, sure, no problem," she grouses as she laboriously sits up. He helps her to stand, then keeps a hand on her because she's not steady on her feet. She fumbles with her pants and then shoes, but when he tries to assist, she irritably waves him away. He can see she's struggling to move so once she's clothed again, he scoops her up and cradles her high against his chest.

She doesn't protest or argue, which tells him how bad she feels. Instead, she just closes her eyes and rests her head against his shoulder.

He likes that she relaxes into his arms, trusting him. "I'll keep you safe," he promises her.

They walk in silence until he feels her start to twitch in his hold. Her heartbeat speeds up, and she starts sweating. When she tenses and draws into herself, he knows her heat is causing her pain again. He looks around for a soft piece of ground to set her down.

This time, he doesn't pull off her shoes, just draws her pants down over her knees and lets them stay gathered at her ankles. Her knees flop open, giving him access, and he doesn't hesitate, drawing her into his mouth with relish.

It takes longer this time, but he doesn't mind. She tries to pull away from him the moment she climaxes, but he doesn't move, keeping her legs trapped under him.

"I estimate it was about forty minutes before you needed another orgasm," he states. "Is that normal?"

"No," she whispers. "Usually, it's an hour or two between. This heat is . . ." She hesitates, then goes silent.

He keeps his tone gentle and coaxing. She's in pain, and he's determined to be patient with her through this. "Please tell me."

"It's never been this intense. Never this strong," she admits with a small sound of distress. "Normally, I have almost a day of warning before it hits. Plenty of time to find a guy or take some drugs. And it's never this painful so soon. It feels like I'm being stabbed in the stomach with hot pokers. That's not supposed to happen until halfway through."

"If I copulate with you, do you think it would be more helpful?"

She gives a short, sharp laugh as she reaches for her pants.

"Probably, but I wouldn't want to inconvenience you or anything."

He ignores her sarcasm and helps her pull up and fasten her pants. He picks her up and starts walking again. They both remain quiet, lost in their thoughts. Finally, she breaks the silence.

"I can't get pregnant," she says in a voice so low it's barely got any sound to it. "So, you don't have to worry about that."

Kilan's surprised, but then again, he could've missed that bit of information being issued from the doctors because he deliberately ignored the daily reports the Council circulates about the Decanted women.

When news of the Decanted women was made public, he was glad for his species, but uninterested for himself. He had his great love and now she's gone. A man missing his heart can't belong to another.

But that doesn't mean he won't take good care of Deena while she needs him.

"That's good to know," he finally says cautiously, unsure how she feels about the fact that she can't reproduce. It won't lessen her value to any Hissa male. By the way all the men in the classes tried to get her attention, there are plenty who would mate with her even if they couldn't have children.

Her laugh is humorless. "I'm sure it is."

They lapse back into silence again. He works to keep his strides long and even, trying to make her journey as smooth as he can. When he feels her tensing, he quickly finds a place to set her down. This time he reaches for her shirt first and she gives him a questioning look.

"I think I should stimulate all your erogenous zones," he explains. "I read a little of human physiology when Mara first settled here with Tiran. I know that your breasts can be very sexually stimulating as well as the skin of your neck and buttocks. I will add stimulating those along with your sex this time. Perhaps that will help lengthen the time between your heat becoming painful."

"That's mighty clinical of you," she mutters and reaches to draw off her shirt. "I can't fault your thoroughness, but you're flirting could use a little work."

Normally, his first instinct would be to show icy disdain at her words. In the past, this conversation would inevitably lead to an exchange of taunts and cruel observations, usually ending when he puts his foot down as her superior, insisting she remain quiet.

It's obvious to him now that she uses sardonic humor and

cutting remarks to drive others away.

You have no place to criticize, he thinks to himself. *You've developed the reputation for being irritable and demanding, then wielded it like a weapon ever since the Decanted women started arriving.*

He doesn't voice a rejoinder. He ignores her tone and takes her comment at face value. "How does one flirt?" he murmurs as he gives into impulse and leans close to her, nuzzling her neck. "Will it help with your pleasure if I learn to speak in an enticing manner?" When she growls with frustration, he hides his smile.

"Just . . . just . . . do something!" she wails.

He cups one of her breasts in his hand, enjoying the weight of it. He squeezes slightly, she reacts, but it's minor so he explores more. Using his mouth, he tastes the skin of her other breast, focusing on the beaded nipple. She hisses out a breath and thrusts her chest out, inviting him to touch her more. With his mouth around one nipple, he moves his hand until his fingers can roll the other nipple, and she moans.

He torments her breasts a little longer and then moves his mouth up until he can kiss and nip at her neck and shoulders. She wraps her legs around his hips and rubs her still clothed sex against him.

"Please," she begs as she pants.

"Tell me what you want," he demands, and she shivers under him. "You have to tell me, or I won't do it."

"More, please," is all she can manage to say. Apparently, he isn't moving fast enough because she digs her nails into his chest. "MORE!"

He pulls back, but before he can reach for her pants, she's already ripping them open and pulling them down. Her hands are shaking, and she's making frustrated sounds deep in her throat.

"Easy," he whispers to her and pulls her hands away from her pants. She lets go of the fabric and grabs for his crotch. She finds the outline of his erection and starts petting him, her eyes completely focused on him now.

"Want," she demands and squeezes hard enough to make him choke a little from surprise.

"Easy," he says again, this time with a little more force and pulls her hand away. He grabs her around the waist and flips her over, putting her on all fours. Then puts a hand on the back of her neck and pushes her head down, forcing her ass in the air. She follows his directions willingly and once she's in position, he can see her natural moisture running down the insides of her legs.

He pushes her legs apart with his own and pulls himself out of his pants, positioning the head at her entrance. He starts to ease inside her, but she has other ideas and almost violently pushes herself back. In one swift motion, she's forced him inside of her, stopping only when her backside hits his pelvis. The sudden sensation of being surrounded by tight, warm, liquid heat makes him gasp.

He wants to mindlessly piston into her but concentrates on her pleasure instead. Reaching around, his fingers find the little bud of nerves between her legs and starts rubbing it. She moans and rocks against him. He leans forward a little and reaches under to palm a breast, pinching the nipple the way she liked it earlier.

Her rocking movements become more frantic, and she starts making a desperate mewling sound. He takes his cue from her rhythm, and as she rocks against him faster, he moves his fingers with more urgency. She screams when she climaxes this time, her soft sheath convulsing around him. It's too much, and he can't hold back his orgasm. He roars as he comes, bringing both his hands back to her hips to hold her in place as he fills her.

"So that's what I've been missing out on," she mutters as she pants under him. "I should've gotten on the Hissa sex bandwagon sooner."

For the first time in more years than he can remember, Kilan finds himself laughing.

CHAPTER

4

Deena wakes up slowly. Her body feels like she was trampled by a herd of Pienters. Everything feels sore and abused. She blinks open her eyes, absently noting that she's in some kind of roughly hewn, stone room, lying on a cot that would be narrow if she was Hissa-sized. She draws off the warm, thick blanket covering her to sit up. That's when she realizes she's naked.

Then she remembers what happened to her clothes and sighs.

It took two days for Kilan to walk the two of them to the shack. At some point during those two days, her clothes were irrevocably damaged. Kilan stripped off his shirt to cover her, but even that was eventually destroyed.

And yet, he never complained.

Forced to carry her weight the entire time, he comforted her with soft words and an occasional kiss. They spent the first night in the jungle in a nice spot he found near a small, porous rock bowl of burbling water and some edible plants. He built a bed for her out of giant soft leaves and never once fell back on the cold cutting comments so plentiful in the past.

The next day, whenever they were forced to stop because the pain of her heat became unbearable, he tried to find the same plant with big soft leaves to make her a bed. On a few occasions, he didn't have time because she waited too long to tell him she needed him. After the second frantic coupling, he admonished her to stop being stoic and tell him the moment her need started to build.

And damn, the man showed some intense stamina. She's never had a partner keep up with her while she's in heat, but Kilan didn't just service her, he made sure to check in on her between bouts of frantic sex. As best he could, he kept her hydrated and fed, despite the jungle's tendency to be less than cooperative. Between carrying her, seeing to her needs, and dealing with the heat every time it spiked, she's not sure he ever rested.

They reached the shack just before nightfall the third day, and her heat broke sometime in the wee hours of the morning. Although exhausted, Kilan insisted she eat and drink before drawing her into his arms and falling asleep himself.

But now she's waking up alone in the tiny one-room building. Could he have collapsed somewhere outside while gathering something for her? She isn't sure if he ate, and she knows he didn't get enough rest. That, along with all the physical effort on her behalf, would render anyone comatose. She needs to find him. Needs to know he's well or help him if he requires it.

It makes her smile despite her worry. She likes the idea of being able to help him in return.

Despite the warm jungle air filtering into the shack from a high, round window, she feels chilled and wraps the warm blanket tightly around her before standing up. Her legs feel unsteady, and she ends up falling backward and lands in an ungraceful heap back on the cot. Some help she'll be.

"That didn't go as planned," she mumbles as she struggles to right herself.

The door bangs open, and Kilan rushes in, followed by several other Hissa wearing matching uniforms.

"Are you well? What happened?" He drops to his knees in front of her. She stops struggling with the blanket and just smiles at him. He's shirtless, and his pants are torn and dirty. He has dirt streaks on his face and chest, and fatigue shows in his eyes. But to her, he looks everything handsome and wonderful. The sight of him fills her with emotion she's not interested in identifying.

"I'm fine," she says, letting herself just enjoy gazing at

him. "I tried to stand up, but I guess I moved a little fast. You wore me out last night. My legs weren't quite ready to hold me up yet."

She watches with fascination as Kilan looks both proud and embarrassed at the same time. "You're not hurt then?"

"Not in the least," she assures him.

"Not even," he glances down her body meaningfully and she blushes.

"I'm fine there. You're big but gentle. Thank you for that. I've never had anyone treat me so well during my heat."

"You deserve all the gentle touches you want," he tells her, reaching up to cup her cheek in his hand. "It was my honor to be the one who cared for you."

She lets go of the blanket, allowing it to drop away from one shoulder so she can reach for him. But before she can touch him, he hisses out a breath and drops his hand away from her as if he's been burned. The blue scale pattern on his head pales as he backs away, staring at her neck.

Hurt, she pulls her hand back and watches him pull away. "Kilan, what's wrong?"

"I can't do this," is all he says, then turns on his heels and practically sprints out of the cabin. The three men that followed him into the shack don't even spare him a glance, they are too busy staring at her, or more specifically her neck.

"They're beautiful," one of them murmurs with a kind of reverence.

"I've seen pictures of them on the other Decanted women, but this is the first time I've seen them in person," another one says with awe. He starts to reach for her, but she slaps his hand away and struggles to her feet.

"Hands off," she barks. She doesn't have time to deal with these guys. She needs to go after Kilan and find out what's wrong. Does he think he hurt her? She might be a little bruised, but that's common. He shouldn't be concerned.

Two of the men steady her as she stumbles up from the bed. Clutching the blanket, she concentrates on staying on her feet. The moment she's sure she can support herself; she shakes off their hands and staggers out the door. Once outside, she turns in circles, taking in the empty clearing around the cabin and the very small hover transport with its doors wide open, giving her a clear view of its empty interior.

Did Kilan just walk out into the jungle?

"My pack is missing," one of the Hissa says as he steps up

to stand next to her. She looks over to where he indicates and sees two identical packs sitting in a row and a bit of disturbed ground cover where a third must have sat.

"Why did he leave?" she whispers, feeling bereft. Had she read the situation that wrong? Was he that eager to get away from her? That sends a sharp pain through her heart, making her fight to keep the tears at bay.

One of the men touches her lightly on the shoulder to get her attention. "Please don't be distressed. I know Kilan. He's a skilled male. With Hurin's pack, he will easily navigate the jungle."

"Geran's correct. My pack is well prepared," Hurin volunteers, stepping up to her other side. "It could support an individual for a week."

She turns to him, trying and failing to keep her voice even. "But he left. Why did he just leave like that?" The men cast mournful looks at each other. She sets questioning eyes on each of them in turn, waiting for an answer. "Well?" she demands, her tone turning harsh.

"Kilan is a damaged male," Hurin finally says. Deena just barely keeps her temper in check.

"If by damaged you mean arrogant, critical, and demanding, I totally agree," she quips, proud that her voice sounds strong. "Still doesn't explain why he went from Mr. Snuggly to Mr. Sprint in two seconds flat."

Geran snorts a laugh and the other two grin at her. "Mr. Snuggly?"

Deena sighs. Of course they'd focus on that. "Guys!" she bellows, making them all stiffen and wipe the humor off their faces. "Answers?"

With a resigned expression, Hurin reaches a hand out intending to place it on her shoulder. She steps away from him before he can make contact. She doesn't want him touching her, even with the blanket as a barrier between them. She doesn't want anyone touching her.

Except maybe Kilan, if he ever gets his head out of his ass and returns to apologize.

"No touching," she scolds. She knows everyone on Hissa reads those damn reports the Council issues. Several of them remind everyone not to touch her unless asked or her life is in danger.

"Sorry," Hurin retreats a step with his hands up. "I forgot.

Please, just go into the building."

"Right, sure, no problem," Deena lies as she walks stiffly into the shack. "What did you want to show me?" Hurin just points to a mirror on the wall, and Deena glances at it, looking away before her brain can register what her eyes saw.

She's about to start in on Hurin when it hits her, and she turns back to the mirror, taking a stumbling step forward and leaning in to better see her neck.

"Pienter shit," she mutters and brings her hand up to trace the mating marks covering the base of her neck and extending out over her shoulders. It couldn't be any clearer to her now why he left her.

Kilan saw them and ran.

Numbly, she turns back to face the men, all waiting silently, staring at her marks with a combination of longing and jealousy. She buries her hurt and anger deep—she's good at that—and gives the guys a tight smile. "These marks fade, right? Couple of weeks and they'll be gone?" All three nod.

"If you don't have intercourse with Kilan again, they will fade away," Geran elaborates. "With Hissa women, they usually faded within two weeks. We don't know about the Decanted females. None have ever been left alone long enough for them to fade."

And yet Kilan couldn't get away from her fast enough. Ouch.

"Great," she declares with a poor imitation of enthusiasm. "I'll just cover 'em up till then. For now, I could use a shower and a hot meal. I don't suppose you guys could take me home now?"

"Medical first, then home," Geran tells her firmly. "They're expecting you."

"Big surprise," she sighs. She can't fault the Hissa for their care. If anything, they're overly protective of all the Decanted women. The concern feels strange to all the women after living lives where very few, if anyone, cared about their well-being. She tries very hard not to find fault with the Hissa on that score, so she trudges to the hover transport. "Let's get this over with."

They let her shower at medical and fed her so she doesn't complain when they start poking and prodding her, asking all kinds of questions about her pain levels. It took hours, but when they are finally done, she's left alone to rest.

Now she's just waiting for the final all-clear so she can go home. She's sitting back on a soft bed with a data pad one of the med techs found for her. She's examining the schematics for a Class G hauler, one of the more common types the Hissa use to ship their minerals off-world.

She's deep into the engine stats when the door opens and her favorite Hissa doctor enters. When she first came to the planet and explained that, unlike all the other Decanted females, she was designed to go into heat, he was the only one that agreed to drug her.

All the other medical staff insisted she find a male to satisfy her needs, or several if necessary. They were further disturbed when she refused with an abrasive commentary that included her opinion of their suggestion. Mender Dimon was the only one who gave her sedation and pain medication without comment. All he asked was she come to him if they didn't work so he could figure out better medication.

She knows he got called before the Council to explain his actions, and he stood firmly on her side, endearing himself to her. So, when he appears in her room, she feels her first genuine smile since leaving the jungle curl her lips.

She puts down the data pad and swings her legs off the bed. "Mender Dimon, it's good to see you."

"Don't get up," he says as he hurries over, pulling a chair with him so he can sit down next to the bed. "I'd have been here sooner, but I just couldn't leave little Firan."

Deena feels a bolt of fear go through her at the mention of Lara's child. "Is she sick?"

"Don't concern yourself. It was a routine checkup. She's a healthy, beautiful baby," he assures her, and Deena slumps a little in relief. "The only thing wrong is her tendency to draw everyone to her. The child just manifests joy wherever she goes."

Deena chuckles. "That's the truth."

"But now I'm here with you, my second favorite female," he continues, drawing a small data pad out of a pocket and tapping on it a few times. "You can leave now if you wish, but I'd like to ask you a few questions for my research on Decanted females."

"Ask away," Deena invites. Mender Dimon is the only doctor who gets her full cooperation.

"Excellent," Dimon enthuses as he looks through a few

things on his data pad.

"This was the first time you went through heat here on Hissa without medication," he confirms, and she nods. "Did you have the same amount of warning time before your heat started this time?"

"Funny you ask that. I didn't have much warning at all. Looking back, I realize I was running a slight fever that morning, but I usually have at least a day between that and my full heat hitting me. This time it was only hours."

Dimon gives her a concerned look. "Interesting. I sincerely hope the medication I gave you didn't cause this."

"It didn't," she assures him. "You didn't give me anything I haven't already used in the past. It must be something on Hissa, maybe a spice in your food or one of the flowering plants in the jungle that finally started affecting me."

"I'll test for those things," he tells her as he taps rapidly on his data pad. "Was there anything else unusual about this heat cycle?"

She thinks for a moment, trying to stay clinical and keep Kilan's face out of her mind. "It was on the short side. It ended just under the normal duration for a short heat cycle."

"Shorter is good. Was it more intense than normal?"

With a grimace she nods again, "Substantially. And the relief between needing didn't last as long. Usually, I can go up to four hours before the cramps start up again, but this time I was lucky to last an hour."

"Everything from your testing says you didn't suffer any damage," Dimon murmurs as he reads something on his data pad.

Memories of Kilan kissing her, holding her, whispering endearments in her ear flash in her mind. "No physical damage," she agrees. *I'm not so sure about emotional suffering though.*

"You've been on Hissa for almost a full human year," Dimon points out. "It's interesting that it's taken that long for something on Hissa to affect your heat. I'm going to look into this and make sure nothing in your physiology is degrading or malfunctioning. When you have time, I'd like you to submit a list of all your activities and interactions between your last heat and this one. Note anything you've done this time you didn't do previously. That might help narrow down anything in your environment that might be affecting you."

"Sure, no problem," she responds. It's an easy task considering all she's been doing for the last six months is training at the flight school. And the last month is even easier because all her training flights have been with Kilan and none of the other instructors. "Anything else?"

"I'd love to bring you back in for samples before your next heat." She smiles again because, unlike the other Menders, she knows this is an actual request, not a veiled order. Dimon must be one of the most laid-back and patient Hissa on the planet. All the other guys should take lessons from him.

"You're my favorite doctor. It's no burden to visit in a few weeks," she tells him, and he gives her a warm smile.

"Wonderful!" he says with a broad smile and stands up. "One of the techs is finding you some clothes. Be nice to him when he shows up with something you won't like. He's young and eager, and his emotions are fragile."

His words make Deena smirk. "I won't hurt his feelings," she promises as Dimon leaves.

The tech with her clothing arrives shortly after. She's disappointed to find the shirt she's given is in the traditional female Hissa style, with a wide scooped neckline to better show off mating marks.

She doesn't feel like being stared at, so she wraps the loose cloak that came with the outfit tightly around her shoulders to cover her neck. It's not perfect because she needs to hold it in place, but at least she doesn't feel so exposed.

Her escort is waiting just outside her room. She's never met any of them before, but that's not unusual. When the Council realized she was more resilient and far more confident than Lara, they let the Hissa soldiers rotate as her guards, so she never gets the same males twice.

She knows every single guard hopes she'll pick him as a mate. She's learned to be polite to the guards, but distant so they don't take her civility for an invitation.

"Take me home, boys," she commands, ignoring the way the two men stare as if trying to see through the cloak to the marked skin underneath. She gives a little sigh, ignores their intense gazes, and marches down the corridor, confident they'll fall in step behind her.

She can't wait to be home, close her door, and ignore everything for a little while. Maybe cover her mirror too, just until the mating marks fade. Some people, like Mara, like to meet challenges head-on. Deena's different. She's not above facing down adversity, but she's also of the mindset that some things are worth avoiding until they go away.

As far as she's concerned, she's earned some avoidance time.

CHAPTER 5

Deena takes a deep, fortifying breath as she steps onto the training field. The marks are finally gone, and she feels comfortable leaving her home. Well, as comfortable as a girl can be when every male that sees her stares, and more often than not, tries to give her something.

In Hissa culture, males offer gifts to the females they're interested in. Females only accept the gifts if they are interested also, so thankfully, the males accept her rejection with good grace. But it distresses her to see their faces go from excited and hopeful, to despondent and resigned.

There are more Decanted women on their way to Hissa. The Council sent out an announcement with names, basic information, and pictures. That takes some of the pressure off Deena, but not much. With over a hundred thousand Hissa and only a handful of Decanted women, competition is fierce. She hopes to be flying soon and distancing herself from most of the males. Even boring runs to the moons and back will give her quiet time on a ship, just her and the stars.

Eager now, Deena breaks into a jog. The Hissa waiting for her next to a shuttle looks startled and hurries over to meet her. "Are you well?"

She waves off his concern. "I'm perfect, Instructor Javir," she assures him. "I'm just eager as hell to fly."

He laughs and moves to lead her to the shuttle. "Although the crashed shuttle couldn't be recovered, we believe it was a failed thruster component that caused your last flight to end so badly," he explains. "The Council was so upset that they sent this for your test today."

Deena examines the shuttle and gives a little whistle. "That's so new it gleams," she comments, making Javir chuckle.

"It was delivered just last week, along with several more for the new fleet. It isn't the small one you've trained on before, but there's no reason you can't pilot this one just as well."

Considering she's piloted things a hundred times the size of this tiny shuttle, Javir's assurances are unnecessary. She shoots him a cocky grin. "Let's get this guy in the air and see what he can do."

Javir nods and follows her into the shuttle. Deena wants to dance with joy when she sees the state-of-the-art control console. The ship even smells new. She takes a deep breath, enjoying the smell of components that are so freshly made they're still outgassing a little, creating that new-ship scent.

Settling into the pilot's chair, she starts running her fingers over the controls, checking to see what kind of hardware and software this shiny new ship comes equipped with.

She is so distracted by this new toy that she doesn't think about Kilan at all for the entirety of her test. The time flies by as she completes each requirement of her final flight test.

"The last thing you need to do is an emergency landing on the far end of the field," Javir tells her. "Start by taking us out of the atmosphere again, simulate a single-engine failure, then come back down and land. For this part of the test, you need to act as if we're flying a large hauler, something freight class. This begins the tenth and last section of this test."

She nods and pilots the ship off-planet. It's the third time she's broken atmosphere during this test, and each time she sees the stars, it fills her both with peace and a deep sense of longing. They both sit in silence as she starts a long, slow, turn-around, pretending she's flying something much larger and more cumbersome.

Once it's done, she shuts down one of the engines and shows that she knows all the procedures and possesses all the skills necessary to handle a partially operational freighter.

"I was told that you and Kilan crashed right after takeoff," Javir comments casually as he taps something on his data pad. "You didn't even make it to the second section of the test."

"That's right," she responds, trying to keep her tone equally casual even though the mention of Kilan's name sends a jolt through her.

"We're all curious. Did you land the shuttle in the jungle or did Kilan take the controls from you?"

She pauses, surprised by the question. "What is Kilan telling everyone?"

Javir shrugs and looks up from his data pad. "No one's seen Kilan since the crash. He's probably still in the jungle." Concern shoots through Deena.

"No one's found him?"

"No one's looking," Javir explains. "Why would they? He took a well-stocked survival pack and deliberately walked away from the shack. Walked away from you. He'll wander back when he's done sulking."

That makes Deena pause. "Sulking?"

Javir gives her a knowing look. "I'm sure you don't need me to tell you that Kilan is a difficult male. This isn't the first time he's disappeared into the jungle. He's one of the only Hissa I know that doesn't like to be around others. Frankly, we were all a little shocked when he claimed you as a student. Everyone knows he isn't interested in finding a female, but he was adamant. Even went before the Council to argue that he should be your only instructor."

"He was? He did?" This is all news to Deena. She assumed he was assigned to her and reluctantly at that. "He's always so disapproving."

Javir chuckles. "He can be a difficult task master and hard to please. We assumed he fought to be your instructor so none of us would bother you while you were going through training. Then you show back up with mating marks only he could have put there." He stares at her expectantly, and she feels herself blush a little.

"I went into heat in the jungle," she tries to keep her tone blasé. "He did what he had to do to keep me comfortable."

"Oh, that certainly explains a lot," Javir comments. "We were all curious, but no one could ask you any questions because you've been self-isolating. I hope whatever made you self-isolate is resolved now. I know myself and many others were saddened by your absence."

Deena absently touches her neck. "I'm good now. I just needed a little time alone because of the crash and dealing with my heat in the jungle. Everything's fine now." She draws his attention to the control console display. "We're in position. I'm going to start a mock emergency shut down of the port engine."

"Carry on," Javir instructs and taps a few things on his data pad. As with everything previously, this section of her test goes smoothly. Javir tells her to fly back to the field and land at her leisure. Although the last landing isn't part of the test, she approaches it as if she's still being judged and does everything by the book. Including performing a quick flyby to verify the landing spot is solid and without obstructions. None of the pilots do this in real life, but she doesn't want to fail because she didn't follow the rules with an instructor onboard.

During the flyby, she's startled to notice a small crowd has gathered near her landing spot. After landing, she finishes shutting down the engines, and answers the last few questions Javir needs to ask her about safety protocols if she has passengers onboard and had to do an emergency landing.

She answers everything as if reading from a manual.

"Congratulations, Pilot Deena," Javir states with a big smile after the last question. "You've passed your flight test. I'm proud to announce you're cleared to fly any Hissa ship except for anything in an active war zone."

"I promise not to pilot a load of minerals into battle," she jokes and then gestures to the crowd gathered outside. "What's going on?"

"Everyone knew you would pass. That's your graduation celebration," he explains. The last thing she wants to do is spend the rest of the day mingling with a bunch of lonely Hissa males, all waiting for their turn to ask her out. But she can see Lara's down there and knows she can't just duck out. Lara's fear of men has gotten much better, but even with her doting Hissa husband close by, she still struggles at times to keep the anxiety at bay. If her friend is brave enough to face a party full of men, the least Deena can do is join her.

"Welcome to the Hissa fleet, Pilot Deena Clanless!" someone shouts out as she exits the shuttle, and a general cheer goes up. She gives them all a big smile and hurries over to Lara and her husband, Selon, before anyone can pull her aside for an intimate conversation.

"If anything proves you love me, it's this," Deena teases her. Lara hands her baby to Selon and reaches out to grasp Deena in a tight hug. Generally, Deena's not too fond of being touched, but she always puts up with it for Lara.

"I'm so glad you finally left the house! I was so worried," she says. When they pull apart, tears are leaking out of Lara's eyes.

"You're one to talk," Deena retorts. "The only reason you leave the house is to go to the repair bay. The only reason you leave the repair hanger is to go back to your house."

Lara gives a little laugh and sniffs. "But that's normal for me. You never stay inside. Never. You're always moving and doing things. I didn't know you could be still for so long."

"Oh please, don't exaggerate," Deena argues. "I spent an entire week on the Anavac homeworld, remember?"

"You got stuck for an entire week on the Anavac homeworld. There's a difference," Lara points out.

"Enough of this," Deena says as she moves to stand in front of Selon. "I need my baby fix. Hand her over!"

With an indulgent smile, Selon gently transfers the gurgling baby to Deena. The little girl looks up at Deena with big happy eyes and gives her a toothless smile. She looks mostly human, except instead of hair, she has the Hissa scale pattern on her head. Unlike other Hissa, her scale pattern is a light red instead of blue and doesn't seem to change color with her emotions.

"You made a beautiful baby," Deena murmurs, transfixed by the joyful child. "Say 'Deena'," she coos at the child. "Deeeennnnnaaaa."

"She's too young to talk yet," Lara says with a laugh.

"Never too young to start learning," Deena counters. "Now little Firan, repeat after me, 'I'll always remember to take into account weather vectors when calculating atmospheric re-entry'. Did you get all that, sweetie?" This makes Selon laugh also, and soon the three of them are chatting about the new role Deena hopes to assume in the Hissa fleet.

Deena stays close to Lara, knowing that all the other males will give the anxious woman a wide berth for fear of causing her distress. Selon helps by providing a physical barrier she can casually hide behind, so it's hard for the others at the party to catch her attention.

All too soon the baby starts fussing, making Lara and

Selon congratulate her one last time, and then leave. Without the small family to act as a buffer, the Hissa all descend on her, most of them fellow graduated trainees or instructors from the flight school.

It's then that she realizes how much Kilan shielded her from the interest of the other males. She always assumed he was just gruff and picking on her, but after the hundredth hand touches her without permission, and none of the other instructors reprimand the males, she sees Kilan's actions in a much different light.

He always acted displeased with her and anyone she talked to. Getting her attention meant males had to risk his wrath. That kept them from seeking her out too often, or invading her personal space, when they were all housed in the same classroom.

But now, with no one telling them to back off and leave her alone, she's forced to retreat over and over again. Her caustic comments that kept others away don't seem to work with these Hissa. They shrug off her abrasive words and crowd her even more. She'll be working with these men, so she doesn't want to alienate any of them. But then a hand touches her butt, and she's done.

She swings around, ready to lambaste the offender, only to find five males staring at her. The hand could've belonged to any of them. She knows better than to ask who the guilty party is.

She looks around for her guards. When she finds them, she starts toward them, forced to push past one guy who refuses to move out of her way. "I'm worn out," she tells the crowd with false regret. "I report to Fleet Leader Misan tomorrow for my first assignment, so I should head home and get some rest."

Words of disappointment fill the air as the guards hear her words and step forward, pushing the crowd away from her and giving her some breathing room. She sends them thankful looks as she waves goodbye to everyone. "I'll see you all later," she calls out, falling into step between her two guards.

"Thanks, guys," she says once they're out of earshot of the party.

"You could have signaled us sooner," one of them mutters. "We weren't sure if you invited the touching or not. We didn't want to interrupt if you were gauging one of the males as a potential partner."

"I probably won't see you guys again," Deena says. "But feel free to spread the word. I'm not into touching. Lara and the baby are the only exceptions. If someone grabs a handful of me, it better be because they're saving my life."

"This will be noted in our report," the other guard tells her. "We'll be more vigilant now that we're aware of your preference."

"And I'm going to find that pilot and make sure he understands not to touch you again," the other guard growls, making Deena smile for real.

"No retribution needed," she assures him. The last thing she needs is an entire group of pilots beaten up because they may or may not have grabbed her ass. "But giving any future guards the heads up would be appreciated."

"My name's Timon," the guard who threatened an entire graduating class of pilots on her behalf tells her.

"I'm Nokin," the other volunteers.

"It's nice to meet both of you," she says. "I hope you end up in my rotation again."

"We're your permanent guards now," Nokin explains.

"But I thought you guys were all set up to rotate so more of you could meet me?"

Timon shakes his head. "Selon petitioned the Council to limit your guards to several sets, instead of a large rotation. He said you struggle with too much attention every time the guards are switched. That it's causing you stress and that might be one of the reasons your heat was more uncomfortable this time. The Council agreed and asked for volunteers for permanent duty. Now, there are three sets of us that will be your guards. No more new faces."

"I bet a lot volunteered," she mutters, and Nokin chuckles. She ignores the fact that all of Hissa gets regular updates about even the most intimate part of her health and well-being.

"Many did," he agrees.

She casts a look behind her at Timon. "How did you guys get to be the lucky ones?"

Timon shrugs. "We don't know what criteria the Council used to choose us."

They reach her house, and Nokin opens the door to allow her inside. She pauses and casts awkward glances at both of them. "Normally, I invite the guards in so they can hang out in the house in comfort," she starts to explain, but Nokin cuts her off.

"You need space, just like Lara does sometimes," he states with ease. "We're going to remain out here until we are relieved this evening. Even if you invited us in, we wouldn't have accepted. You trusted us enough to be honest. Now, go inside and find your peace. Tomorrow will be a busy day for you."

"Thanks, Nokin," she says with sincerity. "Thanks, Timon. I'm pleased you were both selected."

"It's our honor. You should rest now. We'll keep all others away." Timon grabs the door and gently closes it in her face.

She grins at the shut door. She doesn't know why the Council picked these guys, but it seems like they picked guys who not only can keep their hands to themselves but are also willing to close a door in her face. Other guards pushed to be inside the house with her. To talk to her. To interact with her. These two pushed her away, and she adores them for it.

She didn't eat anything at her impromptu party, so she meanders toward the cooking area to see what she has to snack on. All the windows of the house are shuttered, and she doesn't bother turning on the light despite the dimness inside. The lack of light is the reason she doesn't see the figure until he's right on top of her. One strong arm wraps around her chest, trapping her hands to her sides. Another large hand clamps over her mouth, keeping her from crying out for help. She's lifted off her feet and carried up the stairs and into her bedroom. Her struggles don't seem to bother her attacker at all.

Once in her bedroom, the male sits down on the bed with her in his lap, drawing her tightly against his chest. She hears him take a deep breath as he buries his nose in her hair. The move is so familiar that she shifts from abject fear to overwhelming rage.

"Don't scream," a familiar voice whispers in her ear. "I just wanted to talk." When he removes his hand from her mouth, she doesn't scream, she just glares.

"Nice of you to show up, Kilan. Now that I know you're not dead, you can just march your ass right back out of my life."

CHAPTER

6

It's the smell of her that hits him the hardest, even as he steeled himself to see the mating marks again. He thought it would be the feel of her soft body against his that would break him, but he forgot how much her enticing scent affects him. She fills his nose and fogs his brain, and the only thing he can think about is how warm and inviting her body was for those two days he cared for her in the jungle.

"If you don't want me to scream, you're going to need to let go right now," she tells him, her words biting. He's not ready for her to put space between them, although it's the safest thing to do. After today, he might only ever see her from a distance at the port or in passing at one of the receiving stations on Diminish or Brimming. He certainly will have no reason to get close enough to touch her.

Taking one last lung full of her delectable scent, he releases his hold on her. She surges out of his arms as if the touch of him is repugnant. She stomps across the room and slaps the control panel next to the door, lighting up the room and shutting the bedroom windows. She turns to face him, crossing her arms over her chest and scowling. But once she gets a good look at him, her scowl turns to concern, and her arms drop to her side. He hasn't seen a reflection of himself yet but knows he must look ragged and worn.

"You look horrible," she declares and takes a step forward. He thinks she's going to touch him, but she seems to catch herself and draws herself back, keeping her distance.

"I've been in the jungle," he explains. "I walked all the way back from the shack."

Her eyes widen, "With only enough supplies for three days?"

"I'm well versed in how to survive in the jungle," he assures her. "The pack I took contained far more than I needed for my journey."

It hadn't contained a change of clothes or sturdy boots. He'd given her his shirt and within two days, his pants started to show the wear of breaking a path through the indomitable Hissa jungle. Now the garment is more hole than fabric. As for his feet, he's afraid to take off his shoes, knowing his feet are probably nothing but bloody messes of ulcerated blisters. He should have gone to his own home first. He should have cleaned up, eaten, slept, then visited.

But the moment he reached the city, his body marched him to her house. Even though he knew she was taken care of. Even though he knew there was no way she went anywhere but straight to medical by the retrieval crew, something in him needed to verify her health. Needed to know she was safe.

Needed to see if his marks were still around her neck.

"You need to go to medical," she declares, and he shakes his head.

"Not necessary. I'm just dirty. Not hurt."

She eyes him skeptically. "Fine, it's your body," she concedes. "But if you pass out in here, I'm calling in Timon and Nokin to haul you to Medical."

"Consider me suitably warned."

She's wearing a Hissa style cloak that ended up bunched around her shoulders when he grabbed her, and now she reaches up, working it off over her head. He waits impatiently for her to be rid of the garment, eager to see her neck. When smooth, unmarked skin is revealed, he knows he should be relieved, but feels a strange kind of tightness develop in his chest.

"They've faded," he murmurs.

She shrugs and tosses the cloak onto a nearby chair. "You

knew they would," she points out, her voice harsh. "You should be happy now. You seemed upset when they showed up before."

"I apologize for just walking away. I should've accompanied you in the hover transport. It was shameful of me to leave as I did." There, he expressed his remorse, admitted to his shame. He should feel better now. She's safe, the marks are gone, and he's confessed his failings. He should be able to leave.

Should, should, should, but doesn't.

He remains there, staring at her bare neck and then shifts his gaze up to her eyes. She looks away, seemingly studying a stack of clothing in a far corner. "Well, it worked out fine. Thanks for helping me through my heat," she says without moving her gaze back to him. He finds he wants to see her eyes because her voice sounds strangely thick.

"It was my honor to assist you," he tells her, and that might be the first true thing to come out of his mouth since arriving.

"Right, well you won't need to do it again. Dimon is going to figure out why my heat triggered faster than normal and give me drugs to see me through it next time. It's all taken care of."

"Drugs," he echoes with alarm. "Trying to dull your heat with medication seems dangerous."

She finally looks back at him. Her eyes are strangely bright, and her tone is bitter. "Don't concern yourself at this late date. You made it very clear that being with me was traumatizing. I wouldn't want to make anyone else endure it." Sarcasm drips from those last words and Kilan winces. He wasn't thinking of the emotional damage he might cause when he ran away from the shack. He could only think of his overwhelming fears.

"Any male on Hissa would be eager to see you through your heat. There's no need to use drugs."

"Any male but you," she states flatly, and a single tear falls from her eye and trails unnoticed down her cheek. He can't take her pain any longer. Jumping up, he scoops her into his arms and sits back down on the bed, ignoring her halfhearted protest.

"I didn't leave because of you," he murmurs, and he hugs her to his chest. "I left because of me. I'm a damaged male, unfit and unworthy. No matter how many Decanted women are brought back to Hissa, I won't find a mate among them."

She stops struggling and sniffs. "You were so tender while I was in heat. I don't understand why you went back to hating me. The marks don't mean anything. It doesn't mean we have to form a Family Pact together. You didn't need to leave like you did."

He takes a deep breath, letting her scent soothe his chaotic feelings. Then he realizes what he's doing. He can't get attached to this female, and he can't let her develop feelings for him. He needs to be decisive.

"Perhaps it's best that I did," he tells her brutally. "You seem to be confusing my servicing you during your heat for affection." She rears back at his words as if slapped. He starts to say something else, to stab another dagger into her feelings for him, but a voice from downstairs draws their attention.

"Pilot Deena? The smell of an unknown male is very strong in your house right now. I just need you to call out and verify you're well and that this male was welcomed by you."

"I'm in my room," she shouts before Kilan can stop her. "I need an escort." Rapid footsteps sound and the two guards burst into her room, breaking the door in their haste. Kilan pushes Deena away from him, worried she might be hurt if the guards engage him in a physical confrontation. Deena moves away, putting herself behind the two warriors before he can grab her and draw her behind his own body.

"Kilan stopped by, but he's overstayed his welcome. Please escort him out of my home," she commands. Neither warrior moves for a moment.

"Did he hurt you?" one of them asks. "I smell human tears, and your voice tells me you're upset."

"She's fine," Kilan growls out, angry at this male for being so familiar with Deena and furious with himself for caring that he made her cry.

"She can talk for herself," Deena declares with haughty dignity, her voice no longer quavering. "Leave, Kilan. You said your piece. Now we don't need to see or talk to each other ever again."

Kilan tries not to growl when one of the guards reaches out to draw Deena further away from him. "Don't touch her."

"She's ours to guard," he informs Kilan coolly. "You gave her mating marks and walked away. I'll never understand a male like you, but I can only be thankful you thought such a treasure worthless. She's ours now to care for. You no longer have a role in her life."

"I'm her instructor," Kilan says, falling back on the only role he can legitimately claim.

"Not any longer," the other guard informs him with satisfaction. "She passed her test today. She no longer needs instruction. She has no further use for a coward such as you, in any way."

Kilan feels the news like blows to his heart. Someone else flew with her. Someone else tested her skill. Someone else gave her the news she could fly again with the Hissa fleet. That was to be his role, his duty, his delight. One last excuse to see her.

He stands still, letting the pain ease before he tries to speak.

"Very well," he says, falling back on icy disregard. "May the moons bless your travels, Pilot Deena." It's a traditional blessing, but the words feel like ash in his mouth.

"Same to you," she responds, probably unaware that the normal response to his blessing is '*and forever light the night sky*'. Or maybe she does know the correct thing to say and is deliberately refusing to use it.

He can't see her because the guards are keeping their bulky bodies between the two of them. If she wanted to, she could push them aside and face him, but she doesn't. Instead, she stands there, quiet as he strides to the door, passing close enough to one of the guards to bump him harshly with a shoulder.

The guard doesn't respond to the childish action, just waits until Kilan moves into the hall. He hears one of them ask Deena to remain in the room, then footsteps follow him down the stairs and out the front door.

"She bore your mating marks," the guard mentions casually as he shadows Kilan outside. "I never saw them, but I heard from Hurin that they were beautiful. She hid them. She mostly stayed inside while they marked her skin. When she left the house, she covered them up so no one could see. Everyone knew, but she hid them anyway like a shameful secret."

Kilan knows he should just leave. He should ignore the male's taunting words, keep his pain hidden. But finds himself turning around anyway. "She probably just didn't want to be stared at. She wants to be seen as more than just an available female."

"We all know she's more than a potential mate," the guard argues. "She's a female of courage and skill. The male she chooses will be honored. Her young will be clever and strong-willed. She's valuable beyond measure. All of us know these things, except perhaps you. Weak males don't know how to treasure precious things."

With that final blow, the guard turns and walks back into the house, giving Kilan his back as if he's so unworthy there's no need to fear him.

Kilan isn't sure how long he stands staring at the closed door before the pain in his feet and the fatigue in his body force him to make his way home.

CHAPTER

7

Deena stares at the control console display, taps a few items, then sits back and props her feet up just next to the display. The shuttle hums as its maneuvering thrusters start making adjustments for reentry.

"You seem more weary than normal," Timon says, drawing her attention to the co-pilot seat where her guard sits. After several weeks of successful runs to the moons and back, Deena assumed the Council would withdraw her guards. When that didn't happen, she made polite inquires, pointing out that no one was going to attack her while flying a shuttle in the middle of Hissa territory.

The Council responded in one word: miners.

If she hadn't been so annoyed with them, she might have laughed. Every time she does a run to one of the moons, she finds herself eating, drinking, and even engaging in games of chance with the miners. They're a hardy, unrefined group, and she adores their complete lack of deference for the Council. The fact that they willingly exchange verbal barbs with her only makes them more appealing.

She knows it frustrates her guards to no end, especially when she jumps into the more physical games the miners play. But the miners are the best distraction she's found. The flights back and forth from the moons are short and uneventful, her skills only necessary when a rare storm system progresses over the landing field. Hissa space doesn't even have random space junk to avoid, making the journeys painfully boring.

Did she spend months in training for this?

She crashed into the Hissa jungle and spent two days trapped with Kilan for this?

Two pleasure-filled days trapped with Kilan.

With a growl, she shakes her head, trying to banish the cantankerous male from her thoughts. Easier to do when her mind is occupied so she turns to Timon. "I shouldn't have played the jumping game with the miners, even after they made the squares smaller. It wore me out. Don't worry. I've learned my lesson. I'll stick to the less physical games next time."

Timon snorts. "I doubt very much you will refuse if they offer again. You enjoy the comradery far too much. But I don't mean you're physically tired. You seem unhappy. Weary of this job."

Deena sighs. Of the six Hissa warriors that rotate in pairs to guard her, Timon is by far the most observant. "I always knew I'd be restricted in where I could fly, but I thought I'd at least get to visit the colony on Torrind Minor. There's a gorgeous gas giant on the way there and those are the best for slingshots. If you time it just right, you create a pattern in the exosphere." She pauses, thinking fondly about gas giants she visited in the past.

"Your face lights with joy when you talk about such flying," Timon comments. "Fulfill this role without incident for several more months, then approach the Council again." He pauses for a moment, and Deena glances over. The big guard is struggling with what he should say.

"Just tell me," she demands. "If you know something, just spit it out."

Timon gives a little shrug. "My cousin is on the Council. They're trying to decide how to deal with free Decanted females that don't want to come to Hissa. Right now, the general opinion is that they should be forced to come here if they can't be persuaded or bought. But because it's such a severe tactic, there's been a general outcry. We're struggling with our need for females and the sovereign rights of any being to decide their future. My cousin believes they'll reach a consensus soon."

"How does that impact me? I'm already here," Deena points out.

"My brother believes the Council will compromise with an enforced stay of six months, and after that, allow the females to leave if they wish. That's assuming they agree to meet males during their stay. The assumption is that within those six months, they will find a Hissa to mate and want to stay."

"I've been here over a year and a half," Deena murmurs. "Would the law be retroactive? If they pass those guidelines, will I be allowed to leave right away?"

"I would assume so," Timon admits. "But I'd beg you to be patient with us and stay. Your flight duties will be slowly extended as they realize your skill levels. The Council already limited your guards to the six of us. That should show you their willingness to compromise."

"But that was a fight," Nokin comments from behind her. "The military representative in the Council fought hard to keep the rotation going, but Selon made a passionate argument for a limit and Mender Dimon backed him up. Remember how Selon had to make it an issue about health and the strain of interacting constantly with so many strangers? The Council granted the request but only after a very lengthy debate."

That's news to Deena. She thought the request for limited guards was passed without much fuss. Nokin's revelations are just a reminder that everything she does is meticulously scrutinized, not just by the Council, but by all of Hissa.

"You have that weary look on your face again," Timon states grimly. "That wasn't my intent."

"Not your fault," she tells him quickly. "I just spent my youth trapped. It's hard to feel like that again. Unable to make my own decisions."

"It seems to bother you more now that Lara is mated and has a child," Nokin observes, making Deena shrug.

"When she needed me, I had focus. But now she's doing so well, she doesn't need me to protect her anymore. Then the training gave me something to focus on. Now, all I do is milk runs that a well-programed autopilot could accomplish. Especially now that Lara has retrofitted all the cargo shuttles with better thrusters." She glances over at the two of them. "And I know there are some extra rules in place for when I visit the moons. You can't tell me that the other pilots are restricted from going down into the mines, even for tours."

"Your situation is unique. You can't expect to ever be treated like just another Hissa male," Timon states softly.

"So, in the end, your advice is to bide my time and be good?" she asks with a humorless grin. "I guess I can do that. If they don't extend my route I can just wait until—"

She stops talking as a sudden wave of nausea rises up in her. A cold sweat breaks out on her skin, and she clamps her hand over her mouth and scrambles out of her seat. Timon rises to follow her and Nokin steps out of her way as she rushes to the small room that houses the onboard facilities. She just manages to make it to the waste receptacle before she vomits up the lunch the miners fed her.

"You're sick," Timon declares, worry in his voice.

"I'll contact Mender Dimon," Nokin says. Looking up, Deena sees Nokin tapping on a data pad.

"No!" she objects but turns to vomit again, heaving bile into the receptacle. Timon steps forward and places a gentle hand on her back.

"This isn't normal behavior," he points out. Deena draws in a ragged breath, hits the wash function on the receptacle, and lets herself slump back against the wall behind her. Timon crouches down, his face a mask of concern. Nokin stops tapping at his data pad but doesn't look pleased about it.

"Don't tell anyone," she pleads. "It's probably something I ate. It's nothing. Humans have weak stomachs. We void contents all the time, not just because we're ill."

"That is true," Nokin comments, looking a little less worried. "I read that humans might even vomit from pain sometimes."

Deena nods in agreement. The last thing she needs is a visit to Medical and the circus that will ensue if the Council thinks she might be sick. Or worse, if they think the vomiting is caused by her piloting duties. The thought of being stripped of her role in the Hissa fleet, as boring and paltry as it is, makes panic build in her chest.

She stands up determinedly, grabbing Timon's hand for assistance. She's pleased to note that she feels much better now that she's voided her stomach. It probably was something she ate. Those miners like to spice their food far more than the rest of the Hissa population. She probably just imbibed too much of something her stomach didn't like.

"I'll contact Mender Dimon later," she assures them. "I'll talk to him about the stuff the miners eat and just avoid it next time. Problem solved." Neither guard looks happy, but both reluctantly nod their heads.

"Will you tell us what Mender Dimon tells you?" Nokin asks. "We won't put this in our reports, but we'd like to add any food intolerances." She gives him a genuine smile. Nokin is always polite like that, asking instead of demanding. It's one of the reasons these two are her favorite guards.

"No problem," she assures him. A sound from the control console draws their attention. "Move guys," she orders with a wan grin. "I've got a milk run to finish."

The rest of the day goes smoothly. Deena lands without incident, drops off her cargo, checks out of her shuttle, and lets Timon and Nokin walk her home. Sometimes after a day of flying, she likes to go for a walk in the jungle near her house. Several groomed paths weave through the sections of jungle that have all been cleared of dangerous plants. Today she wants to be alone for a while, so claiming fatigue, she retreats to her room.

"You're going to contact Dimon before you rest," Timon reminds her. "You need to speak to him about the food you ate."

"Sure, I'll do that right now," she calls back as she climbs the stairs to her room. She closes the repaired door and slumps down on her bed. She doesn't feel the need to sleep so she fulfills her promise by sending a request for a comm link to Dimon with her data pad. The response is almost immediate: the large display on one of the walls of her room flashes with his symbol.

"Display, allow communication," she says, and Dimon's concerned face fills the screen.

"Are you well, Pilot Deena?"

"I'm perfectly fine," she assures him and then explains what happened on the flight back from Brimming and her suspicions of the cause. She trusts Dimon not to raise alarms over such a trivial incident.

"Curious," he murmurs after she's done. "They use all the same spices as we do here, but you're correct that they use a great deal more per dish. I'll look into it and also run some simulations. For now, I suggest not consuming any more food on either

Brimming or Diminish just to be safe. If you void again, I must insist you come directly to me." It's a familiar refrain and not the first time they've struck this bargain. He'll keep her secrets if she agrees to tell him everything and report in if any issues persist. It's a fair trade.

"Do you know if Mara, Lara, or Mian have suffered any issues with the spices?" she asks.

"They haven't, but they've never eaten with the miners," Dimon tells her with a little laugh. "I believe you're the only one to have that honor so far."

"They're an exuberant bunch," Deena replies with a laugh of her own.

"The fact they haven't eaten with the minors might explain why none of the other women suffered voiding issues. Except, of course, when they're pregnant," Dimon points out causally. "But I'll double check all their food intake and make calculations to be on the safe side."

Deena feels herself go cold at Dimon's words but manages to nod her head and keep a smile on her face.

"Thanks, Mender Dimon," she says, overly cheerfully to cover her fear.

"Of course," Dimon responds. "I'll contact you tomorrow with my findings." The screen goes blank, and Deena just stares at it.

Pregnant?

She was so sure she couldn't get pregnant. After years of being dutifully fucked by her husband but never producing anything, she assumed it was something wrong with her. That idea was cemented after years of using males off and on to relieve the symptoms of her heat that never resulted in pregnancy. She just assumed she couldn't have children.

She looks down at her clothing-covered stomach. Her biosuits have been fitting tighter lately, but she just assumed she was putting on weight. Recently, she determined to start refusing some of the food everyone's constantly offering her or sending over to the house. Anyone might gain a little weight when they're constantly surrounded by delicacies.

But if it's the food, then her biosuit should be tight all over, not just across her chest and belly.

Pregnant!

Panic hits her hard enough to make her feel shaky. If the Council finds out she's pregnant, they won't let her fly anymore.

She'll be stuck planet side. They might even force Kilan to live with her. The idea of spending her days dealing with his resentment is too much to bear thinking about.

She'll never be free again.

She'll have a husband that doesn't want her, again.

She can't let that happen.

She needs to get off-planet and away from Hissa-controlled space, and she needs to do it soon before she starts showing or Dimon figures it out.

She refuses to be trapped in a cage again, gilded or otherwise.

CHAPTER

8

Deena never expected it to be so easy to ditch her guards. But she spent so long being well-behaved during pilot training, and then two months of doing everything according to Council dictates as an active pilot, that there's no reason for anyone to be suspicious of her. It also helps that today Safir and Jolon are on the roster and those two are the least vigilant of her guards.

With no assigned flights for the day, she tells them she needs to visit medical to discuss her next heat cycle with Dimon. She leaves them in the hall as she ducks into his office, knowing the doctor isn't in there because he told her he'd be on Brimming for a few days. She then moves into an attached exam room and out the other side, placing her a hallway away from her guards.

From there, it's easy to make her way out of the building and into a waiting transport, which starts moving the moment she's inside. Mara, already in the transport, hands her a bundle of clothes as Tiran steers the vehicle away from medical. "Put these on," Mara says and starts tugging Deena's top off.

"Window!" Deena hisses, but Mara laughs.

"They're set on tint. No one can see in. Tiran thought of it," she explains and casts a loving glance over at her mate. When Lara and Deena were first rescued by the Hissa military and brought back to the Hissa homeworld, the two of them lived with Tiran and Mara. Although they tried to be polite and accommodating, Deena never got over seeing the happy couple constantly touching, kissing, and gazing deep into each other's eyes. Even before Kilan's rejection, their happiness made Deena jealous. But now it feels like a cut across her heart.

"I thought Selon and Lara were smuggling me out," she comments as she unselfconsciously strips in full view of Tiran. It doesn't matter, the big male only has eyes for his beautiful, black-haired mate.

"She told me," Mara says with a roll of her eyes. "Your original plan wouldn't have worked. Lara and Witch get along well enough, but my sister wouldn't be able to fly her. And everyone knows that, so why would she suddenly decide to take a cruise in her? Hissa males can get tunnel vision when it comes to certain things, but they're far from stupid."

Deena winces. She knew Lara's plan was flawed but didn't have a better alternative. She didn't think these two would be willing to help her. "What's the new plan?"

"Tiran and I'll take you to Minola. It's the closest station where you should be able to buy a ship. Lara said you got the settlement from the insurance for your old ship, Ally. She's giving you her half. And told me to tell you if you don't take it, then she'll find you and 'cry all over you.' Her words, not mine," Mara informs her with a wry expression.

Chuckling, Deena finishes shrugging into the biosuit Mara provided her. "I won't refuse it. She's making good money retrofitting all those Hissa shuttles."

"I already know what you're going to say, but I need to ask anyway," Mara says. "Are you sure you want to do this? You're going to be out there alone. Without Lara. No one as backup. No one to help if something goes wrong."

"I managed alone before I met Lara," Deena points out, ignoring her sense of loss. It will be much different to make her way in the universe without her best friend at her side. And it'll be hard without Lara's technical know-how also. Sometimes, the only reason Ally kept flying was because Lara was so damn skilled.

Alone, Deena will have to trust others to work on the ship and hope nothing breaks far from any planet or station.

"There's a difference between surviving and thriving," Tiran grunts out in heavily accented Space Standard.

"And I'm sure I'll figure out how to go from one to the other, given a little time," Deena tells him with confidence she doesn't feel.

She might be on a path of just survival for a long time. To hide from the Hissa, she'll have to assume a different identity. Her old reputation won't be usable, so she'll have to build a new one. That means taking the shit jobs no one else wants to and being willing to cut her profit margin down to a sliver.

But she's tough. She can do this.

Subconsciously, she puts a hand on her belly. She has to do this.

"Just keep in mind, things might change around here," Tiran states. "Many voices are speaking out regarding Decanted women. Laws and protocols could change overnight. Keep an open mind about returning. Or making us a regular stop on your travels."

He's trying to get her to come back, but it won't happen. Even if the Council passes laws protecting her freedom, there is no chance they'll let her off-world again with a child. But she can't say that to Tiran.

"I'll think about it," she says to placate him. He grunts, clearly telling her he doesn't believe her. The look on his face says he wants to argue the point, but a poke from Mara keeps him silent.

Turning back to her, Mara explains the escape plan. "We cleared our departure with space control. According to the official itinerary, Tiran and I are visiting Beor II for a few days. The waters there are supposed to be good for breeding humans," she explains with a grin and rubs her pregnant belly. "That gives us enough time to get you to Minola and return without anyone the wiser."

"My guards will know I'm gone soon," Deena points out.

"Sure, but they'll be looking all over planet side for you first. They won't even think to check-in with me because they know we aren't friendly," Mara explains cheerfully. "And no one else would ever fly you off-planet or let you leave without authorization. It'll take them days to figure out you got off-planet, and by then, you'll have a ship of your own and be far from Hissa space."

"I bet you jumped at the chance to get rid of me," Deena mutters sourly. She knows she hasn't endeared herself to Lara's sister, but she didn't think the woman disliked her that much.

Mara frowns. "You deserve to choose for yourself," she insists. "We aren't friends, but we aren't enemies either. You kept my sister safe. That means you're family. We might not get along, but you have my loyalty." Deena feels touched by Mara's words and reaches out to put her hand over the other woman's.

"Thank you," she whispers, fighting to keep the tears out of her voice. "That means a lot to me."

Mara gives her a reassuring smile. "The Council is overbearing toward us and being argumentative among themselves right now. They're dragging their feet on creating protocols regarding women who haven't picked mates and want to leave. I understand their motivation, but I don't agree. If no one's captured your heart yet, you should be free to go. We aren't slaves. We aren't owned. They shouldn't be able to force us to stay."

The impassioned speech makes Deena's heart twist a little. The truth is that she did choose, but she wasn't chosen back and the last thing she wants is for her baby to endure a father who doesn't want either of them. No, this baby will know nothing but love. And if she does everything right, no one will ever know she's carrying Kilan's child. The two of them can live as a little happy family far from the Hissa.

Well, live happily once her heart heals.

Shaking off her maudlin thoughts, Deena focuses back on the task at hand, escaping. The transport makes its way unhindered to the port. She wants to demand Tiran drive faster but knows that would just bring unwanted attention to them. When they get to a small ground-to-ship shuttle waiting at the far end of the field, her worry spikes. Several males are moving around the shuttle.

"Stay in the transport until Tiran comes to get you," Mara tells her as Tiran brings the transport to a stop next to a set of large flowering bushes. The greenery gives them cover so none of the men can see Deena huddled in the vehicle as Tiran and Mara get out.

"Hello!" one of the men shouts out at the sight of the couple. "We heard you wanted to take your Witch to visit Boar II. We decided to double-check your shuttle. After what happened to Pilot Deena Clanless during her examination flight, we can't be too careful."

His voice is cheerful, and when Deena pokes her head up to look out the back tinted window of the vehicle, she can see both Hissa males gathered next to Mara and Tiran.

Tiran says something in Hissa, and Mara elbows him. Sighing, he switches to Space Standard, giving Mara an indulgent smile. "It's good to be vigilant," he says. "Especially with this one."

"Hey now, I'm not the one who crashed in the jungle," Mara says with a chuckle. "Witch and I have never crashed or even bumped into anything."

"And yet, trouble seems to find you anyway," Tiran teases her. She rolls her eyes as one of the men speaks up.

"The crash wasn't Pilot Deena's fault," he says quickly, casting a glance at his friend. "Tell them what you found out."

"Oh, it's startling how close we came to losing Deena Clanless," he says with wide eyes. "They finally managed to amass the telemetry data from all the different satellites and then piece together the incident. The failure happened so quickly that it's amazing the two of them survived. If it'd been any less skilled pilots, they probably wouldn't have. I know Mikan who works for Fleet coordination systems, and he's one of the ones that put the timeline of the failure and crash together. He did a recreation, and there's a debate about if it should be made public."

"Why the debate?" Mara asks.

"Because some are worried it will put all the males into protective mode, and Pilot Deena might get mobbed," the other one admits. "I can understand why. It was hard enough for the Council to agree to let her test again. If everyone found out how close she was to dying, they might ground her permanently."

Deena isn't shocked at anything they're saying. She was there. She knows how close a thing their survival was. She didn't know about the debate on letting her fly again, but it doesn't surprise her. A good deal of Hissa would love to lock her away in a house, safe from even the danger of tripping over uneven ground.

The conversation she's overhearing just cements her resolve.

"It might be different when she chooses a male," one of them says. "Once she has someone dedicated to her well-being and protection, the rest of us will be able to relax a little."

"But will she pick a male?" the other questions. "She was reluctant before, and then Kilan was cruel to her, and from what I've heard, she's become withdrawn."

"Kilan," the name is spat out like a bite of nasty tasting food. "I'll never understand that male. The ones that took the hover to them said she looked at him with gentle eyes. How does one walk away from a female who regards him with tenderness and wears his mating marks? It's inconceivable."

"But if she opened herself to the disagreeable Kilan, it's only a matter of time before she chooses another," his friend argues.

This conversation tells Deena that while all of Hissa is on her side, they also see Kilan as proof that her picking another Hissa male is inevitable. They couldn't be more wrong. After Kilan, her heart's been hardened. She'll never make herself vulnerable like that again.

"Whatever happened in the jungle is between Deena and Kilan, not us," Mara says, her voice full of finality.

Both men nod quickly. "You're right. Speculation does nothing but create discord," one says. "We should content ourselves that she is safe and recovered from her ordeal."

"And flying," the other interjects. "I heard that her mental health is much improved now that she's able to pilot again."

"I think Selon should have regular meetings with her. He worked miracles with Lara, he might be able to help Pilot Deena decide on a male."

"Give Deena time, guys," Mara interjects. "This is all new to her. She's spent her life on her own or just with Lara. Having an entire species vying for her attention is startling."

"You make an excellent point," one of them says and drops his gaze to her gently rounded belly. "And how's your young doing today?"

"Are you having any difficulties? We read that Mian suffered horrible stomach pains and voided her stomach often while she carried her young." Both of the men's hands are twitching, telling Deena they're working hard to suppress the desire to touch Mara.

"Active," she says with a laugh. "She likes to kick a lot, especially at night."

Both men brighten at her words. "A female?"

"It's confirmed, my child's a girl," Mara says with a soft smile.

"We can't wait to meet her," one breathes out. "It's good that you're going to Boar II. Perhaps you should spend several weeks there. My mother spent almost the entire last month of her pregnancy with my brother there. As a child, I remember how happy floating in the waters there made her."

"I'm looking forward to it," Mara says.

"But we'll never get there if we continue to chatter," Tiran says with a slight frown.

"Do you have everything you need loaded?" one of the men asks. "Is there anything left in the transport you'd like me to fetch?" His words cause a spike of fear to go through Deena.

"I've already seen to having Witch stocked and ready," Tiran tells them. "It's taken me much too long to convince my mate to visit Boar II. I wanted to be ready to leave the moment she agreed."

That makes the men chuckle. "After she gets there, you might not be able to persuade her to come back here," one says. "May the moons bless your travels."

"And forever light the night sky," Tiran responds. The men shuffle off, and Mara walks onto the shuttle. Tiran pretends to examine the shuttle, taking his time to circle it and poke at things as he mumbles to himself in Hissa. He's doing a great job of looking like he's just being overly cautious. There's a small crowd gathered a respectable distance from the ground-to-ship shuttle, so Deena has no idea how they're going to get her on board without being seen.

Then Tiran walks to the transport and says very loudly, "I'm going to carry you, my love. Please don't argue, it's my right as your male." He opens the door, and Deena gives him a confused look.

"Curl up in my arms and play along," he whispers as he wraps a soft bright blanket around her. "Everyone who watched Mara walk into the shuttle has left. This crowd doesn't know she's already inside."

Nodding eagerly, Deena lets Tiran wrap her up tight and then pull her out of the transport. He holds her tight to his chest and murmurs endearments to her as he carries her onboard. Between the blanket, Tiran's carrying her, and Deena curling herself up in his arms, it must fool everyone because no alarms are raised.

Everything goes smoothly once they're on board the shuttle, and soon they're all safely ensconced on Witch, and on course for Minola station. Since Mara no longer works as a cargo hauler, Witch's insides have been totally redesigned. The old bare-bones cargo area was turned into a large luxurious living space. All the walls have been painted bright colors and soft fabrics are draped over everything.

Picking up a spare data pad, Deena makes herself

comfortable in a soft padded chair in the far corner, away from Mara and Tiran.

After thinking for a bit, she starts recording.

"First thing I need to say is that I'm sorry, Lara. I feel like I'm abandoning you. Even though I know you understand why I had to leave. You've been the most important person in my life for a long time. I'm not jealous of Selon, but I'm so damn proud of you. I'm very sad that I won't get to see your daughter grow because she's just as beautiful as her mama, but I know Selon is there watching out for both of you. I know you hoped deep in your heart that I might pick one of these guys and settle down here on Hissa. We could live next door to each other and raise children together. But I can't do it. I . . . I just can't." Deena pauses as tears threaten to escape. "I know I'll see you again at some point, but not for a long time. I'm not the same person I was, and it's going to take me some time to figure out who this new person is."

She hopes that's vague enough that whoever ends up seeing this recording, besides Lara, won't understand what she means. But Lara will get it. If anyone will get her hidden message, it'll be the woman who's like a sister.

"I thought I'd have days of travel time before I had to say goodbye, but I guess our original plan wasn't very good. Thanks for enlisting Mara and Tiran to help. I promise to send you regular messages, so you know I'm fine, even though we both know I'm more than capable of handling anything the universe has to throw at me. Take care of yourself and that precious baby. I love you."

With that, she ends the recording and puts it in Witch's transmissions queue to be sent in several weeks. By then, Witch will be in orbit around Hissa, and the message won't have any issues getting to Lara.

Feeling strangely numb, Deena curls up in the big chair and closes her eyes. Once she's captain and owner of a ship again, rest might become a luxury, so sleeping now is her best option.

To her relief, she doesn't dream.

CHAPTER

9

Deena settles herself down in the pilot chair of her new bag of bolts. Her ship's seen better days, but it's a well-made freighter that should hold together as long as she pulls into ports to get regular maintenance done. A nearby station pings her ship, and she sends them her ship's identification numbers. With the insurance money, she was able to secure herself a new identification number and the ship but not much more. She's been living on the cheapest nutrient bars she can buy and using a lot of fancy navigating to save fuel.

"We need to buy some decent food," she murmurs to her stomach as a reply shows up on her display. The station is giving her permission to dock and all the standard protocols. "After this contract, we should be able to afford some simulated protein. You're making me crave it, kid, so please don't make me throw it up."

The vomiting only got worse after she left the Hissa homeworld. When she was sick a few times on Witch, Mara sent her some suspicious looks but didn't pry. The only thing Mara asked was that she send long distance transmissions to Lara occasionally to keep her worry and anxiety to a minimum. Deena readily agreed.

She sent the first one from the station she left three days ago. It should be reaching Lara now, assuring her friend that Deena's well but missing the "best mechanic in the whole damn galaxy." Deena hopes that will make Lara smile. Thinking of Lara fills Deena with longing. She's lonely and misses her good friend. Heck, she even misses Timon and Nokin.

"I need you to hurry up and finish in there," she tells her stomach. "I want to hold you in my arms and see your smile. I bet you're going to be even cuter than Lara's baby. But we won't tell her that."

She also needs to earn some extra credits to afford a medical bay when she's ready to give birth. When the family ordered her from the Decanting facility, they specified they wanted a female who would be a good breeder. Her wide hips, voluptuous breasts, and sturdy build are a result of that demand.

Even though she might've been made-to-order as a breeder, it doesn't mean she wants to try something as dangerous as giving birth on her own. No, she's going to need a decent medical facility because she's determined that her baby will have all the advantages she can provide. Including a mother who survives childbirth.

She guides her freighter, dubbed by her as the Gradual for its slow-burning engines, into the berth she's rented for the day. Before she leaves the ship, she dons the disguise Mara helped her acquire. A lumpy robe hides her shape, making her look as wide as she is tall. Then a Galipin hat that obscures her face with its myriad of dangling ornamentation. Finally, the voice box that talks for her, hiding her human tones. The voice box links to a small device mounted behind her ear that picks up sublingual movements of her jaw and turns them into words. It took some practice, but she's mastered talking through it and can now hold conversations with no hesitation or misunderstandings.

It's a cumbersome outfit, but she doesn't have to wear it long, and a bit of discomfort is a small price to pay to keep herself safe. When she left Hissa, there was a rumor going around that some mysterious entity was trying to buy up human women. After seeing multiple contracts for the purchase of human women at astronomically high prices, Deena's made sure to keep a low profile.

Now, hungry, sweating copious amounts in her bulky outfit, and annoyed, she just barely keeps from sighing at the Glonish in front of her.

"I need it there in three standard days," the Glonish repeats for the fourth time. The way his head crest keeps vibrating tells her that he's very anxious.

"And as I said, I can't guarantee that," Deena answers, her voice box making her words even and hides her growing impatience. "It's likely that I'll make it, but if there are any issues, it could take longer."

"But you don't understand, they need to be there for a Nimake ceremony," the Glonish says, his crest moving so fast it's a blur. "If they're not there in time, I'll refuse to pay you."

"Then you can contract with someone else," Deena responds coolly. When the Glonish doesn't say anything, she continues. "I know you did a reputation check on me and found very little history but decided to hire me anyway. The only reason you would do that is because no one else is willing to carry this cargo for you. I have a couple of guesses as to why, but I'm too polite to voice them."

The Glonish flattens his crest against the skin of his head and neck, a sure sign of embarrassment. "There is nothing to guess. There was a misunderstanding with another hauler. It was all resolved to everyone's satisfaction."

"Only one?" Deena asks. The crest waves up once and flaps back down to lay flat.

"Maybe a few misunderstandings," the Glonish amends.

Normally, Glonish are easy to deal with. They tend to be straightforward and business oriented. However, this one seems to be having issues. Glonish don't have sexes, they reproduce asexually. This can create a problem when the newly budded Glonish retains all the memories of being accomplished from the parent who grew them but has none of the wealth or skills to go along with it.

Most newly budded Glonish reprogram their thinking and go out to make their way in the world, but sometimes they end up like this one, trying to do big deals with a reputation they don't have and money they don't possess.

"Here's what I can offer you," Deena states. "I'll do my best to get your Banlder trees there on time, but I can't control the import inspectors or random acts of the Universe. If I'm late, you'll still need to pay me because I'm not guaranteeing arrival in three days. I can tell you that I'm the best deal you're going to get because the offer on this haul is small. And with such a tight time frame, most won't bother, not with what you're offering to pay."

"Fine," the Glonish says, waving its crest in a slow, undulating motion. It's a sign of its resignation. They hold up data bracelets so the funds can be transferred, and a basic delivery contract signed. After she's done with the troublesome Glonish, she hurries off to finish all her tasks so she can leave.

It doesn't take her long to buy what she needs. Then she finds a vendor and buys the largest plate of simulated meat protein she can afford. She scarfs it down in a small communal eating area. When the baby doesn't reject the food, she makes her way back to her ship. By the time she returns to the docks, Gradual is refueled, and her cargo bay is loaded.

She's smiling until she steps aboard, and the smell hits her. She loses all the expensive protein into a trash receptacle and then staggers to the pilot chair, trying to breathe through her mouth instead of her nose.

"Who knew Banlder trees smelled so bad," she gasps to herself as she pings the station with a request for an exit window to leave. "Three days," she tells herself. She's going to get the damn things there in time, not because she wants to make the client happy but because the smell of the things might kill her.

"Only three days to deal with the smell. And I'll never haul these things again."

CHAPTER

10

Kilan waits impatiently for the Council to finish debating about adding a second mining facility on Diminish. He can't believe they're discussing such trivial matters when there are much more important issues to be seen to.

He can't believe the Council is being so complacent with the Decanted women. Who cares if they have enough ore to sell or if the miners need upgraded equipment? The Decanted women are the future of the Hissa species and should always be a top priority. But instead, they are nattering on about quarrying issues.

"Very well," Councilor Natin states. "We'll hire geo-surveyors to map the moon and give us a detailed account of the best place to set up a second mining colony. What is our next order of business?"

Councilor Marun examines his data pad and then casts a disapproving glance at Kilan, who just scowls back, undaunted. "I believe Instructor Kilan wishes to speak to the Council."

All eyes swing to him, most of them filled with disregard, annoyance, or hostility. When the story of him walking away from Deena after she displayed his mating marks got out, Kilan found he had few friends. When Deena disappeared, the animosity of his fellow Hissa only grew. They all blame him for her loss.

It doesn't matter though, because none of them could hate him as much as he loathed himself.

"Council, I wish to know what's being done to find Pilot Deena Clanless," he demands, and the entire Council seemed to radiate displeasure at his words.

"As we've explained to you before." Councilor Natin's voice holds nothing but contempt as he addresses Kilan. "The Decanted female, Deena Clanless, was declared free to leave a month ago. The Council ruled on the rights of the Decanted females, and Pilot Deena resided on Hissa for much longer than the required six months."

"She left before the ruling was passed," Kilan argues. "That invalidates her departure."

"And that's why we searched for her in the time between her disappearance and the final decision. But we have no right to continue to search for her after the new law governing Decanted women was passed." Councilor Natin pins him with an angry glare. "This is the final time we will discuss this with you, Instructor Kilan."

"The law should be revoked," Kilan argues. "They should be forced to stay indefinitely."

Murmuring greets his words. The Council managed to eventually reach a unanimous decision regarding the rights of the Decanted women, but it's by no means a popular one. His fellow Hissa might not be very fond of him, but many agree with his beliefs.

"They're much too precious to the future of our species to let them go wandering around the universe," Kilan argues. "Besides, they're vulnerable, especially with whoever is putting out such high bounties on the capture or sale of human women. Does the Council have such a short memory that they've forgotten how close Mara Lost came to being abducted? If her mate, Tiran, hadn't been there, we wouldn't be waiting for the blessing of her child now."

The crowd of Hissa are no longer glaring at him, the majority of them are glowering at the Council. Kilan doesn't smile in triumph because it doesn't matter. All that matters is that the

Council resume the search for Deena.

"The decision will not be rescinded," Councilor Qulin declares, drawing all their attention. He rarely speaks at the public Council meetings, but when he does, his deep voice commands the attention of even the most troublesome attendee. "We will not become a slave-owning species."

The grumbling stops at his powerful words, and Kilan knows he's lost the momentum of his challenge to the Council.

"I resign my position as a flight instructor," Kilan declares, and a surprised murmuring rises from the crowd around him. Kilan comes from a family of pilots, going through training and passing his flight test at a very young age. He's considered one of the most skilled pilots the Hissa have, which is why they asked him to become an instructor instead of continuing to serve in the military.

"Do you wish to return to your previous position?" Councilor Natin asks. "I know the military would welcome you back to their ranks." Kilan shakes his head and watches Natin's expression turn to one of disappointment.

"I'll be leaving Hissa," he snaps out. "If the Council won't see to the safety of Pilot Deena Clanless, then I will do it myself."

Disgruntled murmurs sound out, and Councilor Marun glares down at him. "You'll do no such thing. Pilot Deena Clanless left not long after her interaction with you. That indicates to all of us that she wants this separation. We can't force you to mate with one of the Decanted women, but we won't allow you to hound one either."

"Then I'm officially leaving to explore shipping and trade contracts for Hissa," Kilan declares through clenched teeth. Everyone's back to glowering at him. He can feel a hundred sets of angry eyes boring into him.

"We can't stop you from trying to expand Hissa's wealth and security," Councilor Marun bites out. "But know this: if you come back here with Deena Clanless, you'll be stripped of your rights and sent to live on Diminish. Do you understand me?"

Kilan meets his gaze unflinchingly. "Perfectly."

Kilan pauses at the door to Lara's workshop. He's not sure of the reception he'll receive from Deena's friend but hopes he can convince her to at least hear him out before she bars him from the repair bay. A dozen Hissa males are working inside, and he can just hear Lara's soft voice giving out instructions or answering questions. Under all of it is the sound of a baby cooing. The wait list to work in Lara's shop was long before she had her young, but it only grew when she resumed her work with her adorable offspring in tow.

In the far corner of the repair bay, the men working for her erected a play area for the child, despite the fact that she can't even crawl yet. It's filled with toys and a large ornate crib. Although the crib might be useful at this point in the child's life, her little body has never been set down in it.

He overheard Lara telling Deena once that the males fight over who gets to hold the baby, even when she's soiled herself and needs to be changed and cleaned. As she works, her baby is passed from man to man, making the rounds of the men that work in her repair bay with her.

To her credit, it never occurred to the kind, gentle Lara to deny any of the big Hissa males the opportunity to hold such a precious burden.

For just a moment, he thinks about Deena growing round with his child but dismisses the thought as fantasy. By her own admission she can't get pregnant, although he never found a word about it in all the reports issued by the Council or medical staff once he started reading everything that he could about her. Her ability to have children is inconsequential. She needs to be found and brought back to the safety of Hissa space. Eventually, she'll find a male to mate with, and even without children, she'll be a valued member of Hissa society.

He's doing this for all of Hissa, he reminds himself. He'll receive no reward for his actions because Deena would never choose him as her male. Not that he would want that anyway. His heart is a broken bit of stone in his chest, incapable of love and tenderness.

"Instructor Kilan?" Lara's voice calls out, catching his attention. "Is there something I can help you with?"

At her words, all the males who were working in the repair bay put down their tools and stand up, putting themselves between Lara and him. His unpopularity displayed in perfect unity. Lara gives an impatient huff. "All of you can return to your work or leave," she states in a quiet voice.

After spending most of her adult life terrified of males, Kilan finds himself reluctantly impressed at her quiet command of the repair bay. Of course, if any of the males upset her, they'll get ejected from their job in the repair bay and lose access to her offspring. That means every single man in the building is always on his best behavior.

All the males return to work, most of them casting him irate glances. He ignores them and focuses on Lara. She's still wary of males so he keeps a respectful distance and forces his voice to remain calm and soft.

"Greetings, Master Ship Technician Lara Star," he says. "Pilot Deena Clanless could be in danger, and I need your help." He's hoping this statement will make her more receptive to his request.

He's not prepared for the cool smile she grants him. "She might be, or she might be perfectly content. Neither situation is your concern any longer, Instructor Kilan." She spits out his title like it's a bad word.

"Not any longer," he says, and she gives him a confused look.

"Not any longer what?"

"I'm not an instructor any longer. I've given up my role. I'm dedicating myself to something else."

Lara's expression turns curious. "Is that something else the pursuit of Deena?"

He remains silent. He can't say the words, or the Council will use it to deny him access to his ship. They could even bar him from leaving Hissa space. Everyone knows what he plans to do, but as long as he doesn't declare it, they can't stop him until he returns with Deena in tow.

"You hurt her very badly," Lara tells him, her voice thick. "Deena doesn't let many people in, and she gave you access. You don't deserve her."

"On that we agree," he says simply. He doesn't deserve anyone.

"She isn't Tarim," Selon says as he steps up behind his mate. The wide neck of his garment shows off the tattoos he received on their mating day. The tattoo is an exact copy of the mating marks that circle Lara's neck. Kilan forces himself to meet the man's eyes instead of staring with envy at his tattoo, the visible symbol of their love and commitment to each other.

"Tarim is long dead," Kilan responds in clipped words. "She has no bearing on the current situation."

"I think she has a lot to do with it," Selon retorts without heat. He comes up behind his mate and wraps his big arms around her. She makes a contented sound and leans back against him, her face relaxing.

"Who's Tarim?" she asks.

"A dead female," Kilan snaps at Lara and he hears the males around the hangar stop moving. If he's not careful, he'll find himself forcefully escorted out of the repair bay. Lara might not be as fragile as she once was, but she still suffers from anxiety and doesn't respond well to any male aggression. Her crew of mechanics are more than ready to intercede on her behalf at a moment's notice. Considering how much everyone seems to dislike him, they'd probably relish the excuse to cause him injury.

"Was she your mate?" Lara asks, and he shuts his mouth before he starts using words that might upset her.

"I know you've received communications from Pilot Deena," Kilan bites out. "I need to know the origination point."

"No," Lara says simply.

He's surprised. "She hasn't contacted you at all?"

"I didn't say that," Lara taunts. "I meant no; I won't tell you either way."

"Don't you want your friend to be safe?" he persists. "She kept you safe. Wouldn't you want someone to keep her safe?"

"Who's Tarim?" she asks again, and he shakes his head. He can't talk about her, not even in exchange for information about Deena.

"We all suffered loss during the Great Death," Selon says gently. "You weren't alone."

"I have no wish to talk about a dead female," Kilan repeats harshly. At least he doesn't have to worry about upsetting Selon. "I'd much rather discuss the living."

"But the dead are still present," Selon argues. "Some of us are still linked to them, letting them pull us away from the land of the living. You breathe, and walk, and talk, but are you actually with us?"

"Enough of your mind games," Kilan lashes out. "I'm not here to have imaginary wounds lanced."

"You should be," Selon says mildly. "Of all the males who've never come to talk to me, you're in the most need." Kilan doesn't have time to decipher Selon's cryptic words.

"Will you help me or not?" he asks Lara impatiently, aware that the males in the hangar have all started to edge closer to him while trying to appear engaged in work. They're just waiting for a signal from Lara to get their hands on him.

"Who's Tarim?" she asks, but this time there's a kind of knowing in her eyes. Kilan heaves out a sigh.

"She's a female I grew up next to. We were children together before the Great Death," he tells her. His words are the truth, but far from the whole story. He sees pity flash across her face, as if she's filling in the story he hasn't told. It makes him angry. She has no right to pity him. She can't possibly know the real horror.

"I'm not sure what you think you can accomplish," Lara tells him. "Deena is slow to forget transgressions. And she seldom trusts, so if you break her trust, I can't imagine she'll ever forgive you."

"This isn't about me," Kilan insists again. "I just need to know she's safe."

"I heard the decree from the Council," Selon mentions casually. "You'll be imprisoned for life if you bring her back here. And it might be for nothing. The Council will just let her leave again."

"It doesn't matter," he insists. "She'll be safe for that time period."

"And her temporary safety is worth lifelong incarceration?" Selon asks.

Kilan glares at Selon for asking such a stupid question. "Of course it is. Her safety is worth more than my life."

"Oh," Lara says quietly. Tears are brimming in her eyes, and Kilan feels panicked.

"Don't cry!" he commands. "They'll toss me out if I make you cry."

Lara waves a hand. "It's just new mom hormones." She blinks a few times and pulls one of her mate's arms up to her chest, hugging it to her tightly.

She points a finger at him and tries to look fierce. "Don't be mean to her," she orders him. "If you find her, you need to be patient and nice, no matter what she says. And don't you dare force her to do anything. Just talk to her."

"I can't promise to be nice," he says through clenched teeth. "But I can promise to be civil."

For some reason that makes Lara smile. "That sounds like something she might say." Her simple words hit Kilan hard. "The last communication I got from her was from Euron Station."

"I'm not familiar with that station," Kilan admits, elated to have this vital piece of information.

Lara gives a little sigh. "I probably shouldn't tell you this, but Euron isn't that large and the only thing that goes through there regularly are parts for building or maintaining terraforming machines. If she was there, it's probably to haul between there and a planet being terraformed."

"Thank you, Master Ship Technician Lara, first mother of the family Star," Kilan says with sincerity. He turns to leave, but she calls his attention back.

"Kilan, I can't tell you about her past. But you should ask her about why the people who ordered her, asked for her to be created with the burden of a heat cycle."

Kilan nods at her once then turns around and strides out, disregarding the mechanic's words even before he's out of the building. Her history isn't of importance. Only finding her and keeping her safe is important.

CHAPTER

11

Deena isn't wearing her costume because Cabeel Station is one of the biggest and most heavily guarded stations she visits. No one gets attacked, robbed, or kidnapped on Cabeel. Drinking and gambling are heavily restricted, and all business transactions must be done in specialty rooms where complex programs monitor all the vid feeds for threats.

Cabeel might be the most expensive station she stops at, but it's nice to walk around without wearing her cumbersome disguise. The last haul almost wrecked her ship when she had to make a difficult landing on a small moon, so she's here getting a few repairs done. There's no spare money to spend, but it's still enjoyable to wander from display to display and look through the wares on the shopping promenade.

Her biosuits are uncomfortably tight now and she's going to need to buy a few larger ones soon, so she makes her way to a seller to price out various suits.

"Pilot Deena Clanless!" a voice shouts out from across the promenade. She turns to find two unfamiliar Hissa striding toward her, their faces joyous. Her first instinct is to run and hide, but that's ridiculous. There's no way she could outrun them. Besides, Cabeel security won't let them force her anywhere. She's safe for the time being. She just needs to make sure they don't identify her ship.

"We never thought to meet you," one of them says as the two crowd around her. "I'm Durin. I'm a pilot too."

"He's the worst pilot in our squadron," the other one declares. "My name's Viton. I'm the best pilot in our squadron. I was involved in the Talerianal battle. Let me purchase you a meal and I can tell you about it."

Deena blinks as the two of them chatter, trying to talk her into eating with them, or going back to their quarters so they can show her their awards and give her gifts. When she imagined accidentally bumping into a Hissa on a station, she assumed it would be a fight for her freedom instead of a return to the familiar courting she was surrounded by on their homeworld.

"Move away from Pilot Deena Clanless," a new voice commands. "You're crowding her and making her uncomfortable with your uncontrolled behavior."

The voice belongs to a third Hissa male she's never met. Although he isn't any taller than the other two, his air of authority and strength make him appear bigger. He walks with a slight limp and there's a scar that travels from his forehead, over his eye, and down his cheek. That eye is milky white and although it tracks with the other one, it appears unfocused. She doubts he can see through it.

"Apologies Section Commander Mavito," Viton says quickly as both the males back away from her.

"Are you well, Pilot Deena Clanless?" Mavito asks gently. Adding an O at the end of a Hissa name denotes that the individual did something stupidly heroic. Most only get the O added to their name posthumously. This Section Commander isn't just an authority figure, he must be a hero as well.

"Pilot Deena Clanless?" he inquires, and she realizes she's been staring at his scarred milky eye.

Embarrassed, she nods her head quickly. "I'm healthy and safe," she promises, knowing those are the two most likely things a Hissa might worry about regarding a Decanted female on her own.

"I'd like to speak with you," he says. When the two pilots

try and speak up, he casts them a hard look and they quiet. "You appear to be shopping, Pilot Deena Clanless. I can accompany you as you walk the promenade. Would that be acceptable?"

"I'm not going back to Hissa," she blurts out, expecting at least condemnation from Mavito if not outright frustration or anger. Calmly, he just nods his head, as if he expected her to say that.

"Of course not. You left for a reason," he responds, his tone mild. He looks over to his pilots. "You two can report back to the ship, and you'll keep the fact that you saw Pilot Deena Clanless to yourselves until we've left the station," he orders. They both give him outraged looks.

"Section Commander Mavito," Durin protests. "We have as much right to woo Pilot Deena as you do."

"I'm not wooing," Mavito counters. "I'm going to verify her health and safety, and then I'll join you on the ship. She won't be leaving with us." The pilots look mutinous, but Mavito doesn't seem concerned. He just keeps eye contact with the men until they drop their gazes.

Before they go, both of them push data cards into her hand so she can contact them. Still glaring at Mavito they walk off, mumbling to each other about the general unfair state of the universe.

"Shall we?" Mavito asks as he indicates the next shop. She walks slowly, and he shortens his stride to accommodate hers.

"We were all sorry you left," he begins, and she stiffens.

"I had my reasons," she says, trying to forestall any argument he might make for her to return.

"And they were good reasons," Mavito assures her. "You were hurt by one of the most bitter of us. Then, when you needed to throw yourself into a task as a distraction, they gave you nothing that would challenge you. A child can pilot the route between the moons and the planet, your skills were wasted there." That's the last thing she expects to hear.

"You're right," she acknowledges. They reach the next shop but don't go in. Standing outside, she pretends to examine the items displayed just outside the shop's entrance.

"If you ask him, I'm sure Kilan would say he has no friends," Mavito says, his voice taking on a mildly amused tone. "But I consider him a friend. We were in the same squadron and saw battle together. He's the best pilot I know, outside of myself of course." Deena chuckles even though Mavito is talking about

Kilan. Just hearing his name is like a stab to the heart.

She likes Mavito, so she doesn't retort with an acidic comment. "I'd rather not discuss him."

"But I'm afraid we need to," Mavito says with a sad little sigh. "Because unless I'm mistaken, you're carrying his young in your belly."

Deena feels herself pale. Mavito grabs her when her legs don't want to support her anymore, guiding her to a nearby bench. "Easy little mother," he says as he helps her to sit. "You're safe."

She grabs his arm, terror making her grip strong. "Don't tell," she begs. "Please don't tell the Council. They'll force me to go back. They'll tell him. I can't—" Her voice breaks.

"Shhh," Mavito covers one of her hands with his own, seemingly uncaring that she's digging her nails into his skin from fear. "I won't tell the Council. For now, your secret is safe." He gives her stomach a pointed look. "But soon it will be apparent to everyone, not just observant Section Commanders. And you'll need care; trained doctors and others to support you."

"I'm saving credits for a medical suite," she explains quickly, trying not to think about how few credits she's managed to save so far.

"Your young is Hissa," he points out. "You need to be among us. It's the right thing to do for the child." Her heart stutters at the thought of returning to Hissa space and seeing Kilan again. She can't face him. And she selfishly doesn't want him to know about their child. She's determined to keep her baby safe, even from the disregard of the child's own father. She opens her mouth to beg Mavito again, but he shakes his head before she can talk.

"I'll strike a bargain with you, Pilot Deena Clanless," he offers. "I'll keep my silence if you stay in contact with me. You have months before the child will need help greeting the world. I'll give you some time, but in exchange, you'll send me regular communications. And I'll need to know where you are at all times. Otherwise, I'll just follow you back to your ship, wait for you to undock and leave Cabeel space."

The implication is clear. Outside Cabeel space, she's vulnerable to capture. Hissa Section Commanders control large battleships with thousands of souls under their command. It would take no effort on his part to collect the slow-moving Gradual. He's offering her just a few months more of freedom. With those months she can plot and plan. When he decides it's time for her to be taken back to Hissa, she can be ready to disappear again.

"I accept," she whispers, and he smiles gently at her.

"Excellent. Now let me buy you a meal. I wish to feed your young, which means I need to feed you." She doesn't bother to argue with him. Despite the knot in her belly from fear, she needs to eat and can't afford to turn down free food. Pride is reserved for those with credits in their accounts.

"Thank you, Section Commander Mavito," she demurs, keeping her eyes cast down as he leads her to the food section of the promenade. She listens with half an ear as he talks about his mission and how she can remain in contact with him. She doesn't let his words bother her. She's already planning her next move. He might have her cornered for now, but she'll make sure it's not for long.

CHAPTER 12

Kilan curses as he leaves yet another terraforming installation. No Deena and no one willing to talk to him about the pilots and haulers that deliver there. He's hit yet another dead end, and he's running out of educated guesses to investigate. Pretty soon, he's going to be forced to just start visiting stations at random and hope to get lucky.

Pushing out of his chair in one violent motion, he paces the confines of the control room, fighting his frustration. If he's too emotional, he won't be able to think clearly and that means Deena spends more time alone and in danger.

The control console display flashes with a request for communication from the Hissa warship Steadfast. He knows many of the pilots that serve on that warship, but he has a feeling it's not any of them that are trying to contact him. After the way he left Deena in the jungle, not too many of his fellow Hissa have been interested in speaking with him. At least not in a friendly way.

"Open communication," he orders the computer, and Section Commander Mavito's face appears.

"Greetings," Mavito says, deliberately not using any titles. Kilan put himself in a strange gray area with his withdrawal from teaching and isolation from the fleet. Technically, Mavito could fall back on one of his older titles, but his comrade in arms is sending him a very clear message with the first words he speaks. Kilan is acting irrationally and not fit to bear any honorifics.

Irked, Kilan gives the male a sardonic smirk. "Mavit, it's been a long time." Mavito doesn't react to the overt insult of Kilan dropping the "o" from the end of his name, instead, he just tilts his head a little and regards Kilan thoughtfully.

"You're not far from our position," he comments. "You could dock and join me for a meal."

"I could," Kilan agrees.

"But you won't, because that would take up precious time you could be spending looking for Pilot Deena Clanless," Mavito continues.

"Something you should be doing," Kilan bites out, losing the tenuous grip he has on his calm. "With your resources it would take only days to find her."

"She doesn't want to be found," he points out, and Kilan almost roars at those words. He's heard them so often now they enrage him. Mavito continues as if Kilan isn't glaring daggers at him. "The Council declared her free to leave Hissa. I would think you of all people would be glad to see her gone."

"If the only reason you contacted me is to taunt me, I have better things to do with my time," Kilan grounds out. Before he can order the computer to end transmission, Mavito speaks.

"I've seen her."

With his heart in his throat, Kilan leans closer to the display. "Where? How long ago? Did you see what ship she was flying? Do you have her Ident?"

"No concern or questions about her health?" Mavito's voice is soft, but his face is hard. "You focus on the wrong things, Kilan. You always have."

This time Kilan does roar. Leaning forward, he punches a smooth section of the control console, denting the metal and making the display image waver before it returns to focus.

"I need to find her first, then I can assess her health! Don't any of you understand that! She's out there alone and vulnerable. Anything could happen to her. She needs to be protected."

"We can't always protect those we love," Mavito responds, and Kilan pounds his fist into the console several more times.

"Don't you think I know that?" he screams. Mavito remains silent, his milky eye glinting from some light reflecting off it. Even before the battle that left him scarred and with a limp, Mavito possessed a penetrating stare. Now, with the way his damaged eye seems to glow, it feels supernatural.

"Perhaps you need to do more than know this fact; you need to learn to accept it." The warrior's face is gentle now. "You hold yourself at fault for Tarim but—"

"Because it was my fault," Kilan cuts him off.

"It was a disease," Mavito reminds him. Kilan doesn't argue with him further. This male knows what happened with Tarim. He should understand that it was more than the disease.

"If you have nothing important to impart to me, this conversation is over."

Mavito gives him a disappointed look, and then the display goes blank. Kilan stands there, cradling his rapidly swelling knuckles, and just tries to breathe through his rage. He needs to think. He needs his reasoning skills. He didn't survive countless battles by giving into his emotions.

If Mavito saw Deena, then it would've been at a station the Steadfast was docked at. He could contact Hissa Fleet Control and request the itinerary of the warship, but it would be a slow process and he might not be granted the information. He can't think of a single male on his homeworld that would help him at the moment. But he's not without resources.

Sitting down in the pilot's chair, he starts searching the limited database he has on this ship. Pulling up the crew roster for the Steadfast, he searches until he sees a name that might prove sympathetic. It only takes a few minutes of communications with the Steadfast to be put in contact with Laxon.

"Kilan," the male says with surprise when he answers the comm link request. "You're not a face I expected to see."

"I have a great need of your help," Kilan admits. "I was told the Steadfast put into port and encountered Pilot Deena Clanless. Can you tell me which station?"

Laxon is silent for so long that Kilan wonders if the transmission is frozen. Just before he's going to disconnect and re-request a comm link channel with Steadfast, the gunner sighs.

"You're a male of honor," Laxon tells him, his face heavy with indecision. "Despite what everyone is saying, I know you wouldn't have treated a female like that. I'm sure you didn't abandon her with fresh mating marks around her neck. There must've been something else going on." Kilan remains quiet, feeling dishonest by not correcting the gunner, but also desperate to have an ally in his hunt for Deena.

"I only want to bring her back to the safety of our homeworld," Kilan assures him.

"Many of us don't agree with the Council's refusal to retrieve her. We're sure she can find a male she deems worthy among us, but only if she can meet us. The crew found out she was on the station long after we departed. There was almost a mutiny. Section Commander Mavito put a dozen males in the brig and sent several more back to homeworld to be tried by the Council for insurrection." He takes a deep breath, his eyes full of worry and his body tense.

"Pilot Deena Clanless is a smart and laudable female, but she's out there alone. This is unacceptable. I can give you her exact coordinates, but you need to promise me something."

"Anything," Kilan says without a second thought.

"If you can't talk her into returning to Hissa, make her travel to Cen Station. We'll be there in a month, and we'll be staying for several weeks. There are thousands of us on the Steadfast, all warriors, all honorable. She can choose from among us. Promise to do this for me, and I'll give you her exact location and the locator numbers of her ship."

Kilan sucks in a harsh breath. The thought of Deena potentially being wooed by thousands of males makes him feel like his skin's on fire. He wants to rage against Laxon, tell him that Deena wouldn't be interested in any of the Steadfast males. Besides, remaining in space, even onboard a station like the Cen isn't an option. This idiocy needs to end. The only place she'll be going is back to the Hissa homeworld.

He'll see to it that she returns to Hissa, even if he has to put her in chains. The crew of the Steadfast might attempt to keep her protected, but no space station, no freighter, not even a battleship is enough to truly make her safe. Only Hissa homeworld with its many layers of defensive satellites and strong military presence is enough to ensure her security.

Just managing to hold onto his temper, he gives one violent nod of his head. "I give you my word. If I don't take her back to Hissa I'll bring her to Cen."

"I'll transmit the coordinates," Laxon tells him and leans forward. Kilan thinks the male's about to shut down the display when the expression on his face turns mournful. "I don't know what happened in the jungle, but I do know that if she picks you, she's chosen a male of value." With those words, his image disappears and the coordinates along with her ship's name and identification numbers appear on his navigation console.

"I wish you were correct," Kilan murmurs to the blank display.

Pulling up the coordinates Laxon sent makes his fear spike. What is Deena thinking? She's right on the edge of a warzone. As he watches, the beacon that marks the location of her ship disappears. There're only two reasons that would happen: her ship was destroyed, or she deliberately disabled her beacon. He refuses to believe the first and knows the second means she's heading to the station deep in an active warzone.

Setting the engines to burn hard, he thanks the moons that he's not too far away. The station might be declared neutral territory by both the warring sides, but that doesn't give him much comfort. Neutral zones have a high probability of being attacked no matter what the combatants agree on.

As he pushes the engines as hard as he dares, he prays to every deity of every species he knows that he'll reach her in time.

CHAPTER

13

Hampered by her bulky costume, Deena makes her way through a crowded thoroughfare toward the port office. Normally, she wouldn't come anywhere near a station in the middle of a warzone, neutral or not, but the contract the station was offering to transport basic supplies was just too good to pass up. She needs all the credits she can get if she's going to make a run from Mavito before he can tell the Council she's pregnant.

She's been dutifully checking in with him, until yesterday. Knowing he wouldn't approve of her current location; she sent a garbled message hoping he would think she was having comm problems. Disabling the beacon that he put on her ship was riskier, but those things fail all the time. If she's quick, she can get her ship unloaded and undocked before he ever finds out she was here, and if he comes looking for her, she'll just show him the broken beacon and ask for another one. She made sure to disable it in a way that it will appear to have suffered from a manufacturing failure.

Now all she needs to do is find the port office, close the contract, get her payment, and hightail it out. Because this is the only working station in the sector, it's so crowded she can hear the bio systems working overtime to keep the air scrubbed. The stink of too many people jammed together makes her wish she didn't have a sense of smell. Her anxiety and frustration increase with every few steps. She's constantly forced to tug her unwieldy garment out from under someone's foot, and the general mood on the station is that of disquiet. It's making her want to move faster than her disguise will allow. If she hadn't seen a contract for human women on the boards at the entrance to the docks, she might be tempted to discard the costume in favor of speed.

She's so busy cursing under her breath as she pushes others out of her way, she doesn't notice the faint buzzing sound. When the floor under her feet starts to vibrate, she freezes, as does everyone else around her. Everyone stops talking as they collectively listen to all the station engines fire at once, pushing the station hard. The only reason to do that is to move the station out of orbit, which makes no sense unless . . .

Alarms sound throughout the station, and the crowd around her goes from still and silent to active and screaming. Deena gets knocked down immediately and can't do anything but curl up into a ball and wait for the panicked traffic around her to clear.

The station's under attack. So much for being neutral.

She needs to get back to her ship. Hopefully, the dock workers successfully fueled it while she was making her way to the port office. Even if they didn't, she doesn't have a choice but to board her ship and flee. If she's on the station when it's captured, she's a prisoner of war at best, food at worst.

The pounding of feet around her lessons, so she strips out of her costume and gets to her feet. Her ankle crumples under her, sending her back down to the floor with a sharp cry of pain. Right, no help for it, she's going to need to crawl back to her ship.

Before she can even flip over to her hands and knees, strong arms are suddenly around her, lifting her up to cradle her against a muscled chest. Instinctively, she starts fighting.

"By the moons woman, stop hitting me!" a familiar voice growls out, and Deena looks up to see Kilan's glaring face. "I'm rescuing you, idiot female. Stop making it harder." Because he's carrying her away from her ship and he called her an idiot, she pops him one more time in the face. He tightens his arms on her and roars. "I said stop!"

"My ship's that way," she points toward the smaller berths on the port side of the station.

"But my ship is this way," he counters, but before he can stride any further, an explosion rocks the station and emergency doors slide closed, blocking them from the larger, more expensive docks he was heading to. He curses and looks down at her. Fear makes her hand shake as she points to her dock.

"Hurry," she whispers. "Before that dock is compromised too."

Without another word, he breaks into a sprint. Deena wraps her arms around his neck and tries to hold on as best she can. They run past the doors just as they start to close.

"Berth 44," she shouts, and Kilan runs in the direction of her ship. He doesn't hesitate when he reaches the ramp, just dashes up, turning just inside the ship so Deena can slap her hand on the display next to the hatch to close it.

The sound of a blaster fills her ears and Kilan howls in pain, dropping to his knees. Deena rolls out of his arms and looks up to see a stranger holding a blaster on them. He looks to be a Regarian, big, hairy, brutish, and holding the small energy weapon with confidence. He must have gotten on her ship to steal it only to realize he wouldn't be able to get past the locks on her control console.

"This your ship?"

"Put down the blaster, and I'll get us out of here," Deena offers.

"Get us out of here, or I shoot you too," he counters. She glances down at Kilan who's dropped to his side, panting. The blaster round hit him high and to the side on his back. Not a fatal wound, unless he's left to just bleed out. She needs to deal with the bad guy and then get Kilan help.

"Right," she says with a nod. "I'm just going to make my way to the pilot's chair. Don't shoot me," she tells the Regarian. As she crawls past Kilan, she grips his hand, trying to comfort him. "I've got this," she whispers to him. "Just be still and try not to let all your blood leak out." He says something to her, but his voice is too soft for her to hear.

Worried her ankle won't hold her weight, she decides to just crawl on hands and knees to the pilot chair. The Regarian follows her with a nasty smirk.

"You're human, right?" he comments and nudges her with

a toe. "You guys are in real demand right now. The Hissa have contracts to buy any of you that come up for auction, and there's someone over in the Degoya system that's willing to pay too. If you behave, I'll make sure you survive to be sold." He pauses and watches Deena awkwardly get herself in the pilot chair. She knows better than to say anything to antagonize the Regarian. His species are known for their short tempers and violent tendencies. She's amazed he was even let on the station. Regarians tend to get themselves banned just about everywhere.

"The contracts for humans say alive and whole, but I could always have a little fun and tell them I bought you that way." She doesn't respond to his taunt, just initiates the start-up procedures for the engines. The Regarian stands next to the chair, blaster aimed at her. "Don't try and fly us to Cen or Wint," he warns her. "There are warrants out for me on both those stations."

She nods and starts plugging in a course that would get them free of the station and nowhere near Cen or Wint stations. Her hands are shaking as she programs the navigation system. A ping tells her that the engines are warm and ready, so she fires the maneuvering thrusters and gets them away from the dock as quickly as she can without doing any damage to the ship.

Outside the station is chaos. There are a dozen warships and thousands of fighters battling it out. She's not sure, but she thinks she might even see the Hissa warship Steadfast in the mix, which doesn't make sense at all because the Hissa aren't involved in this war.

Using a massive freighter as cover, Deena manages to keep the Gradual out of the line of fire. The participants of the battle aren't interested in the fleeing civilian traffic, but they aren't doing much to try and keep them safe either.

Suddenly, she and the freighter she's using for cover are surrounded by Hissa fighters. Well, that answers that question. It is the Steadfast out there and she has no doubt the only reason they're here is to save her dumb butt.

"What are they doing?" The Regarian demands, glaring at the fighters as they clear a path for her.

"Escorts," she answers brusquely. She doesn't have time to comfort her abductor because she's fighting with the controls of her ship. One of her maneuvering thrusters is responding sluggishly so she's forced to compensate with another.

I promise that if you get us out of here, I'll buy you a whole new thruster assembly, she silently tells the ship. *I won't be cheap and just replace the gimble.*

"Well, that's convenient, I can just sell you off to them. I'll need to get rid of that other Hissa though. Don't want them getting upset 'cuz I shot one of their own," the Regarian says as he turns.

Fearing he's about to kill Kilan, Deena throws all power in the starboard engine and maneuvering thrusters, violently twisting the ship. She grabs the pilot's chair as she feels herself lighten from the abrupt change in course, and the Regarian goes flying.

She practically falls out of the chair and scrambles on hand and knees toward her kidnapper. He's already sitting up when he sees her coming at him. Snarling, he brings up the blaster, aiming at her head. At this distance, there's no way he can miss her.

I wanted to meet my baby, she thinks before there's a roar and another body barrels into the Regarian. The blaster goes off, missing her and spending its energy into the nearby bunk. Alarms sound as the bedding on the bunk smolders but doesn't catch fire. There's very little on a spacecraft that can catch fire, so she's not concerned.

Fearful, she watches as Kilan wrestles with the Regarian. The beast is bigger than Kilan, but not by much. Even with the wound, the Hissa manages to get on top of the Regarian, pounding him with big fists. The beast slashes Kilan, digging deep gouges of flesh from his chest and abdomen. Kilan doesn't even seem to notice as he pounds the beast until it goes limp.

With a roar of triumph, he staggers to his feet, grabs the murdering bastard, and drags him to the air lock. Deena watches with wide eyes as Kilan shuts the airlock and flushes the body out into space.

He turns to look at Deena, opens his mouth to say something but collapses into an unconscious heap without uttering a word.

CHAPTER

14

The first thing Kilan's aware of is muted voices. He fights to open his eyes. It takes much more effort than it should.

"He's waking up." That's Deena's voice and it sounds excited. There's a hand holding his, and it tightens. It's a small hand. Deena's hand. He closes his fingers around hers. She's safe. The Regarian is dead. He gives up trying to open his eyes.

When he floats toward consciousness again, the hand is still there, but the voices are gone. This time, it's easier to open his eyes, but the sight that greets him takes him a while to figure out. The walls are the uniform gray of all Hissa military ships, but the configuration of the wall is wrong to be a cabin or office. There are displays everywhere and different kinds of scanners hanging from the walls and even one on the ceiling above him. A display next to him shows a live scan being constantly refreshed, the murmur of his heartbeat issuing from the display is the only sound in the room.

"Hi, big guy," a familiar voice says, making him turn his head. "Are you going to stay awake this time?"

Kilan doesn't talk as he turns his head to the voice. He uses the limited ability of his impeded brain to examine Deena for injuries. She's wearing a medical monitoring shirt, usually used for only the most critically ill patients. The sight of it sends a shockwave of panic through him, and he reaches out a hand and tugs at the long sleeve of the shirt.

"Hurt?" he manages to croak out. She looks confused for a moment; then her forehead smooths as she realizes what he's asking.

"I'm not hurt. I just have to wear this for a little while," she assures him. "You saved me."

"Regarian?"

"You killed him," she explains. "I guess you don't remember much. Let me tell you, you're quite the badass, Kilan. Do you remember getting shot?"

Too tired to talk any longer, he nods his head. He remembers the jolt of the blaster round hitting him in the back and then the intense all-consuming pain. The last thing he remembers is lying on the floor and trying to breathe through the agony as the Regarian ordered Deena to pilot the ship.

"Right, basically you were able to get up despite spilling most of your blood on my ship's floor and tackled the Regarian. Then you pounded him unconscious while he shredded your chest."

Kilan brings a hand up to his chest. He can feel sections of uneven skin where new skin was grafted and is now growing into his existing skin. There are a lot of uneven patches that run the length of his chest. When he touches his abdomen, it feels like there are more patches than original skin. He must have looked like a bloody piece of meat.

"And if that wasn't badass enough, you dragged the ugly, thieving bastard into the airlock and flushed him into space. Damn, Kilan. I've never seen anything like it." He smiles at her words and lets his eyes drift closed. There's silence for a moment; then he hears Deena take a deep breath.

"You saved me, you scowling bastard. You risked your life to save me," she states, her voice thick with emotions. "No one's ever done that before. Stood between me and danger with no weapons and no armor."

He needs to explain to her that she's worth dozens of him. That she's much more important than he is. That she's always been important, not just to the future of Hissa but to his happiness. He wants to make it clear to her that he would claim her as his own if he was a worthy male and not a mate murdering coward.

"You matter," is all he manages to get out. He hears her sniff and her hand on his tightens.

"You matter too," she says, the conviction in her voice no less strong for being spoken through a soft sob.

He manages to utter two words before his brain shuts down again. "Be safe."

The unique and wonderful smell of Deena fills his nose as he opens his eyes, grateful to find he can think clearly. He shifts his head slightly and looks down to find Deena curled up on the medical bed next to him, her head resting on his chest, with one arm and one leg draped over him. She's sound asleep, her mouth moving slightly but no sound coming out. He wonders what she's dreaming of when the hand resting on his chest shoots out and grabs empty air.

"No," she cries out. "No, don't." The hand keeps trying to clutch something, so he puts his fingers in her grasp.

"Easy," he whispers to her. "Easy. You're safe."

"Please don't leave me," she sobs out. "I'll do anything. Please don't leave me." Is she dreaming of him when he left her in the shack? Anguish rolls through him.

"I'm here," he tells her as he pulls the hand clenching his fist to his chest. Her grip is tight on his hand, and she makes a soft whimpering sound deep in her throat. "I'm not leaving. You're safe."

"It hurts," she sobs. "Please Gregor, don't leave me like this."

A shock of anger goes through him. He props himself up on one arm, still gripping her hand with his. "Whose Gregor?" he growls out, and Deena startles awake.

She blinks up at him, her eyes are slow to focus. "Kilan?"

"Whose Gregor?" he asks again, and she shakes her head.

"No one," she replies, sliding her gaze away from his. "He's no one. I was dreaming."

Before he can demand she tell him more about her dream, she looks back at his face, and her expression transforms from wary to excited. "You're talking!"

He gives her an exasperated look. "I've been able to talk for a long time," he points out. "My mother told me I was an early speaker."

She laughs and gives a little shake of her head. "No, I mean you're talking in complete sentences now. This is great."

Her enthusiasm makes him frown. "How long have I been in medical?"

She wiggles a little so she can sit up, and he slumps back on the bed. She smiles down at his supine form and reaches out to cup his cheek in her hand.

"Today is day four. Your color is so much better. The blue in your scale pattern is back. I don't know what was worse, how pale you were everywhere, or the way you kept twitching and crying out in your sleep."

"Four days?" he croaks out.

Hissa medical technology is advanced. If he's been mostly unconscious and in medical for four days, his wounds must have been grievous. He vaguely remembers waking up several times and going back to sleep when he was sure Deena was safe. Never would he think so much time passed between bouts of consciousness.

"Mender Riton, the senior doctor on board, said if you'd gotten to Medical even a minute later, you wouldn't have survived," she whispers, and he sees her eyes glitter with unshed tears. "I can't imagine," she starts to say but can't seem to keep talking. To distract her from her sadness, he's tugging at the med shirt she's wearing.

"Why are you wearing a Medical observation shirt? Where you hurt?"

Her face colors and she looks down at the shirt. She sighs, and her shoulders slump. "I guess there's no time like the present to tell you."

A shock of fear goes through him. "Are you dying?"

Meeting his eyes, she shakes her head. "Nope, not dying. Not even close. I'm pregnant."

Kilan's sure he didn't hear her correctly. "What?" His question comes out much sharper than he meant it to.

"I'm pregnant. You're the proud, or rather unwitting, father. Sorry about that. I honestly thought I couldn't get pregnant." She shrugs and tries to smile, but it falls flat, and she ends up looking mildly ill.

He voices the only thing he can think of. "Mine?"

"Great," she mutters. "We're back to one-word sentences again. Yup, it's yours. Or maybe you guys have super sperm that can impregnate a girl from a distance. Barring that, it has to be yours because your dick's the only one I've ridden since getting mixed up with the Hissa."

Kilan knows he should ask her more questions. He should make sure she's eating enough and resting. He should consult with the menders on board to find out the status of the fetus and Deena's general health. All these thoughts swirl around in his head, but he can't seem to concentrate on any single one of them to act. Instead, he lays there, staring at her with a dumbfounded expression.

"Pregnant," he repeats. "Mine." Wrapping his mind around those two concepts is taking all his brain power.

"Maybe you should go back to sleep. That way, when you wake up, we might be able to have a whole damn conversation," she gripes and maneuvers her legs off the bed.

"No, don't leave," he says and reaches out. She moves her arm away from him and slides off the bed. An alarm sounds, and three Hissa rush into the room.

"Everything's fine, guys," she tells them. "Kilan's awake and talking, mostly." None of the three males bother even glancing over at him.

"But are you well?" the first one asks. "We told you not to walk on the ankle yet."

"I'm completely fine. Same as the last time you rushed in here because I sneezed," she retorts, but that doesn't make any of them back away or leave. "And Mender Riton said the ankle is all healed, and I need to walk on it, so don't pick me up or I'll tell him you're not letting me get better."

"I won't pick you up, but let me just check the baby," another one says and reaches for a scanner on the wall. Deena puts her hands on her hips.

"The baby's fine, just like the previous three dozen times you've scanned me in the last few hours." She tugs at the medical shirt. "What's the point of wearing this thing if you're going to scan me all the time anyway? The tech in this shirt updates you on my condition constantly. The scans aren't necessary."

"The medical shirt can only detect basic things, but the scans tell us much more. And the scans only take a moment," he whines, and the other two males nod emphatically.

"Let me get you a seat," another one says as he rushes across the room to carry over a small chair covered in padding.

Kilan finds himself perplexed at the odd chair. It looks like a standard ship chair that's been covered in bunk padding and then covered again with a piece of bright yellow fabric. The male who grabs the chair practically shoves it under Deena, almost making her fall back against the bed. "Please sit. Rest."

With a sound of irritation, she flops down onto the chair and crosses her arms over her chest. "I'd like to go to my room," she comments. "So, if we could get this over with that'd be great."

A fourth male appears in the open doorway, a frown of concern marring his features. "I heard a noise. Is there anything wrong?"

"Kilan woke Deena up," one of the three males in the room complains and casts a disparaging glance over at Kilan.

The new arrival looks at Kilan with a frown. "Deena needs to sleep and rest. The baby is taking a lot out of her, and with no male to care for her, her body quickly became depleted," the new male tells him, and Kilan knows it's an accusation as much as an explanation.

"Guys, I'm right here," Deena announces loudly. "You know I can hear everything you're saying, right?" Kilan watches as none of the men acknowledge Deena's words.

"Telin, she wants to go to her room," the man who got the chair tells the male in the doorway.

Telin nods eagerly. "Finally! I didn't think she'd ever leave this one's side." The tone and dismissive gesture toward Kilan makes him realize his popularity hasn't improved. "The room's been ready for ages. I'll go over and make sure the temperature and light settings are still optimal." Telin disappears out of the doorway, and Kilan turns his attention back to Deena who's scowling ferociously at the three males hovering over her.

"You know 'that male' you guys keep dismissing saved my life. You're the one who had to carry him to Medical, Wilox, remember? Blood everywhere?" she asks with an aggressive swipe of her hand.

"It's the least he could do," Wilox answers dismissively as he tugs the medical shirt up to reveal Deena's rounded stomach

My child's in there, is all Kilan can think of when he sees her belly. The thought makes him immobile, wrenching long-buried emotions to the surface and forcing him to turn off his feelings to keep from being overwhelmed.

"Wilox, we talked about this," Deena protests and tries to slap his hands away from her. "Ask before you touch." Her voice might be hard and sharp, but Kilan can hear the undercurrents of anxiety.

"This won't hurt," Wilox assures her as a second male grabs her by the wrists and forces them onto the armrests of the chair.

"Damn it, Hirin, let go!" Deena demands, tugging against his hold.

"Easy," Hirin soothes her. "Let Wilox check the baby, and I'll let go. Then we'll take you to your room and away from this one."

With a resigned sigh, Deena stops struggling and lets her head fall back on the chair. "Fine," she mutters. "Just hurry up."

"That's good," Hirin murmurs encouragingly. "Just stay relaxed. No one's going to hurt you." He looks over to the third man in the room. "She should probably eat. Do you think we have any more of the floranish? It seems to be one of her favorites."

"I'll go check," the male says and hurries from the room.

"I'm not hungry," she mutters under her breath but doesn't open her eyes.

Kilan watches the whole scene unfold before him. He should be grateful that this crew is taking such pains to care for Deena. Her every need is being seen to, despite her objections. And yet, watching Deena's protests being ignored as they hold her down to do a painless scan makes him feel ill at ease.

They aren't hurting her, but her body language screams defeat. Her voice should be strong and commanding, not anxious. Her expression should be obstinate, not resigned. This is not the Deena he knows at all.

From the moment she started training with him, she was nothing but fiery enthusiasm and determined energy. Although he made a show of disapproval every time she took a glider out without permission, he secretly enjoyed the look of rapture on her face at the end of her illicit flights. No matter what measures he put in place to keep her from flying alone, she found ways around him and never cowered in the face of his reprimands.

But the woman sitting in the chair seems only vaguely like the arrogant pilot he knew planet side. This version of Deena is stripped of joy, zeal, and sarcastic vivacity. What's left is a woman who looks like Deena but has given up.

Then it hits him. This is what Deena looks like when she feels conquered. This is the version of her denied any hope of future freedom. This is what she looks like when she knows access to flying, even in the sky over Hissa let alone among the stars, is something she'll never get to do again.

Being held down in a chair, even gently, is a physical manifestation of what she expects for the rest of her life. Being pregnant with his child means she'll never leave Hissa again, even if she doesn't accept another male. The Council will ground her and put her under heavy guard for the rest of her life. A bird with clipped wings kept in a gilded cage.

"The baby is healthy," Wilox announces as he removes the scanner and tugs Deena's shirt back down. She doesn't move as Hirin releases her wrists and straightens up. The old Deena would've jumped up from the chair. She wouldn't have liked these two males looming over her. But this new Deena slumps down in the chair, draws one leg up, and wraps her arms around it.

"If you'd like to rest, Manal and I can get you settled in your quarters now," Wilox tells her as he hangs the scanner back on a nearby wall. "Many of the crew came forward with beautiful cloth and other items for your quarters. The room is beautiful."

"As beautiful as we can make a cabin on the Steadfast," Manal interjects. "But there are already preparations underway back home. A house is being prepared for you and the child. It'll be perfect."

Deena doesn't react to anything they're saying. Her expression is far off and sad. She stands up at Wilox's gentle urging and doesn't protest when Manal and Wilox each take an arm, as if she's so frail she might not even be able to manage walking on her own. Kilan thinks she looks a little worn out, but nothing that would require this level of care.

She casts one last look at him, her eyes pleading. She wants him to intercede. The males mated to the other Decanted women are often given great leeway with their females. The Council trusts that a mated male with young will do everything in his power to keep them safe. But without a male of her own, Deena is at the mercy of the entire Hissa population, and none of them are listening to her.

When he doesn't speak up, she gives a little sigh and lets Wilox and Manal half drag her from the room, Hirin close behind. The sigh almost breaks him. That small sound just about cracks open the iron control he's kept on his memories and emotions almost his entire life.

He can't be the male to mate her, he reminds himself. He's unredeemable. He's without honor. Besides, she's safe now. Every male on the Steadfast would willingly put himself between her and danger. And he's sure they're on their way back to Hissa. Once she's in Hissa-controlled space, she's safe from attack or kidnapping. The baby will be celebrated and cared for just as avidly as the mother.

And yet he can't get the thought out of his head that her body might be safe from outward dangers, but she's slowly dying from the inside.

CHAPTER

15

The sound that rings out from her cabin door tells her someone's requesting entrance into her room. She wants to refuse but knows better. They'll come in no matter what she says, and if she refuses, it will probably mean a trip to medical.

She's been sitting at a small display looking at star charts for the last few hours, content to lose herself in memories of places she's visited and fun times she had with Lara. But apparently, her reminiscing time is over because someone needs to check on her. At least they gave her a couple of hours on her own. That's an improvement over the checks that normally happened every twenty minutes throughout the day.

"Enter," she calls out, expecting to see Wilox or Manal, the two medical techs responsible for her. There are a dozen males assigned to her: guards, medical techs, and caregivers. And all of them seem to need access to her almost constantly so it comes as no surprise when Velom, one of the guards and the male in charge of her security, strides in instead of one of the med techs.

"Kilan is requesting to see you," he explains, disapproval radiating from him. She thought her feelings were hurt when Kilan abandoned her after their interaction in the jungle. But it turns out he angered everyone with his actions, not just her. The fact that he didn't know she was pregnant, he couldn't have known, doesn't seem to matter. All the males she's interacted with since coming aboard the Steadfast have either refused to even say his name or mutter despairingly when he's mentioned.

It probably saved Kilan's life that the medical team didn't know who they were working on when he was first brought on the ship. She tried to point out repeatedly that Kilan risked death, both on the station and then later on Gradual to save her. No one bothered to listen to her. According to many males on Steadfast, giving up his life is the least he could do for her.

Apparently, regarding the Decanted women, the Hissa have no forgiveness in them, even for one of their own.

Sitting up straighter in her chair, Deena gives Velom a humorless smile. "Let him in."

Velom's expression darkens "Is that wise? You're pregnant and shouldn't take unnecessary risks."

"He almost died protecting me," Deena reminds him. "I don't think he's going to hurt me."

"Perhaps not physically," Velom agrees. "But—"

"Let him in," Deena orders, cutting Velom's protests off. The look of displeasure on his face tells her that Velom plans to refuse Kilan entrance if she doesn't, so she thinks fast. "If you let me see him, I'll eat the menormor you're always putting on my plate."

"You should eat it anyway," Velom argues. "My mother ate plates of it when she was growing my sister. She said it's the reason her children grew strong within her. Don't you want your daughter to grow strong within you?"

"She'll grow plenty strong without me needing to eat a vegetable that smells like rotting meat and feels like I'm chewing old chair cushions," Deena retorts. "But I'll eat some at my next meal if you let Kilan in."

"Two servings," he counters. "One with midday meal and one with last meal."

"Agreed, but you have to cook it," Deena bargains. "Otherwise, I'll wear out my teeth trying to gnaw through it. I'm Deena Clanless. I don't want to be known as Deena Toothless."

"You exaggerate," Velom says with an expression that

would be more appropriate if she asked him to cook babies for her dinner. "But I'll have it cooked, even though it's better raw."

Grumbling about stubborn women, he walks back out, and then Kilan appears, stumbling into the room from the shove Velom must've administered. The guard follows him in and stands at attention just inside the open hatch. Deena knows better than to try to get Velom to leave. It took her several days to convince the guards she couldn't sleep with them in the room with her. Leaving her alone with Kilan would be out of the question.

"Go away," Kilan demands with a glower.

Velom glares back. "No."

"He won't leave so you might as well just talk," Deena explains wearily. As good as it is to see Kilan up and moving, looking healthy and whole, she doesn't have the energy to act as a referee between these two Hissa.

With a grunt, Kilan turns his attention back to her. She expects him to sit on her bunk or remain standing to loom over her. What he does instead is sink to his knees on the floor just in front of her chair, so she's looking down at him. He's close enough that she could reach out and touch him but doesn't. Of course, he doesn't reach out to touch her. Why would he? Touching her is a burden he never wanted.

Suddenly, guilt swamps her. It wasn't his fault that the shuttle crashed, and her heat come on so suddenly. The mating marks and the pregnancy were all highly improbable and now it seems all his people despise him. Her part in this was unwitting, but it all still happened because of her. It hurt her when he left. It hurt her when he rejected her. But he never claimed to have wanted her to begin with.

He made her no promises. They're both victims of random acts of the universe and circumstance.

"I'm sorry, Kilan," she says simply, fighting the urge to touch him.

Velom sounds a disapproving grunt. "This one doesn't deserve your charity."

"This one's name is Kilan," Deena retorts. "And if you can't keep your mouth shut, you can leave." As she expects, her words have no effect. Velom doesn't leave and doesn't stop talking either.

"You wouldn't have left if he hadn't abandoned you," Velom counters. "You let him touch you. His mating marks were around your neck. And now you carry his child. All these things and yet instead of devoting himself to your care, he turns his back. He threw away a prize of unparalleled value. You ran away from us because he hurt you. You could have been killed. An invaluable child of Hissa would've been lost. All because of him. He doesn't deserve any emotion but contempt. But now you're a treasure we will all care for."

Over the last few days, she's heard different versions of this same speech many times from every male she interacts with. At first, she tried to reason with them, get them to see her instead of just a pregnant, unmated, Decanted female. Eventually she gave up. None of them are even remotely interested in listening to what she has to say.

"I'm not a prize to be won," she snaps at him, fighting to keep from screaming. The Hissa on the Steadfast aren't interested in seeing her as anything but a victim. And worse, they believe she needs to be protected, even from herself. Nothing she says will change their view.

"This is what you feared would happen," Kilan murmurs. His words bring her attention back to him. He doesn't seem angry, which is a surprise considering his reputation for being bad-tempered and irritable. She's so surprised by his calm, contemplative expression that it takes a moment for his words to register.

"I wasn't ever going to pick a male," she agrees, both of them ignoring Velom's sound of distress. "I wasn't ever going to sleep with any of the Hissa. If we hadn't crashed, none of this would've happened. My only goal was to bide my time and eventually leave."

"But now you can't," he comments, dropping his gaze down to her belly. She wraps a protective arm around herself.

"Now I can't," she agrees. They both lapse into silence for several minutes.

Kilan breaks the silence, his tone still contemplative. "They treat you like a beloved but recalcitrant pet."

Those words make Deena smile briefly. "That's an accurate statement."

"It won't change," he predicts, and the little spark of humor she felt vanishes.

"No, it probably won't," she acknowledges.

"Would you pick a male now?" he asks. There's no jealousy in his question, and Deena feels her heart break all over again.

"No," she whispers, fighting back the tears that form much too easily these days. "I already picked."

For the first time Kilan shows emotions, but his expression of disbelief isn't flattering. "You went into heat. You didn't have a choice."

The silent debate with herself doesn't last long. She's wanted to tell Kilan her secret ever since the holo-conference with Dimon when she was first brought aboard Steadfast. But she couldn't tell him while he was in and out of consciousness, and then, well, it wasn't the right time.

"You triggered my heat," she states boldly. "Mender Dimon had Tiran create a program that examined my cycle and my activities. There was a very clear pattern. I started entering into heats more rapidly once you became my instructor. The adrenaline of the crash and your closeness set off my heat in the jungle. If it'd been anyone else stuck out there with me, it probably wouldn't have happened. He thinks that's why you were able to get me pregnant when my . . . when no one else could in my past. I'm not infertile. My body was waiting for you."

Shaking his head as if in denial, Kilan's next words are barely above a whisper. "It is all my fault."

Regret fills her. "It's no one's fault," she insists. "A lot of stuff had to happen, had to go wrong, for us to end up here." She waves her hand to indicate both the Steadfast and Velom standing silently by the door, glaring daggers into Kilan. If she thought the man didn't like Kilan before, he's positively murderous toward the pilot now.

Leaning forward, she gives into impulse and touches Kilan's head, running her hand down the smooth scale pattern from the point where it starts in the middle of his forehead and back to where it disappears under the neck of his shirt. He closes his eyes and doesn't pull away. That fills her with hope. Maybe, someday, they could be friends. She wants her child to know her father.

"I liked you too much," Kilan announces softly after she's run her hands over the top of his head and down the back of his neck several more times. "The moment I saw you, I liked you too much. I knew I didn't deserve you, but I wanted you all the same. I decided I could be content protecting you during the training program because you were so clearly unimpressed with all the males around you. I thought that would be enough, to serve you in that way. Training and protecting you was the excuse I gave myself to be near you. I fought with myself every day of your training. I wanted to touch you. I wanted to lean in and fill my lungs with the smell of you. You'll never know the battle I waged every time you were within arm's reach."

Shocked at his words, she just stares down at him with wide eyes. "But you were always so impatient with me. You barely seemed to tolerate me."

"I thought if I was disagreeable, you wouldn't pick me. I didn't realize you never intended to pick any male. I was selfish. During training, I could keep you to myself. For those months, I was the most important male to you. I was more harsh than necessary because I didn't want either of us to get attached, but I couldn't hand you off to another instructor either."

"What are you saying to me?" she demands. "What are you trying to tell me?"

"I can't be your mate," he tells her, his voice monotone despite the brutality of his words. She's about to react violently when he continues. "I can't be trusted. I'm not a worthy male. I failed a female before. I don't want to fail you."

She takes a deep breath, blinking rapidly as tears build in her eyes. His actions are starting to make sense to her now. It seems that she's not the only one affected by past events. Not the only one making decisions based on old trauma. The tears she's been fighting to keep back start flowing down her cheeks.

"What if I don't care about your past? Isn't that my decision—" she starts to ask when Velom interrupts her.

"This is enough," he declares and strides forward. He reaches down and hauls Kilan to his feet. "You're upsetting her by seeking absolution. This is shameful Kilan, even for you."

"No," Deena protests, standing up and grabbing Velom by the arm. "Stop it. I want to talk to him!"

"Calm yourself," Velom orders and then calls out through the door. "I need a med tech in here."

Pulling himself free from Velom's grasp, Kilan tries to turn back to Deena. "I'll petition the Council to be your sole caregiver," he tells her. "Then I can make sure you're allowed to fly. I can—"

He can't finish his statement because several sets of strong arms close around him. Deena gives a little gasp as Velom and another guard start dragging him backward out of the room. He struggles, but when a third man enters the fray, he's reduced to gasping for air as blows land on his freshly healed body.

"Stop it!" she screams and rushes forward, intent on pulling the men off of Kilan. "Stop hurting him!"

Before she can mount an offensive in defense of Kilan, hands grab her and pull her toward the bed. "Please don't struggle," Telin begs. "Manal is on his way with something to calm you, but you need to stop struggling. You could hurt yourself."

The words do not affect her. Her entire focus is on Kilan being pulled from her room. Telin picks her up and sets her on the bed, easily subduing her until Manal arrives with a drug gun in his hand. She knows it won't do any good, but she continues to struggle anyway.

"Please," she begs. "Don't do that. I just want to talk to Kilan. He wasn't hurting me. The tears don't mean anything. Please don't!" she screams the last words as Telin presses the drug gun to her neck. The effect is almost immediate, and she feels her limbs grow heavy. Telin lets go of her and raises her shirt so Manal can run a scanner over her belly.

"Everything's fine," Manal announces to the others, but if Deena could talk, she'd vehemently disagree with him. His face lights up and he reads something on the scanner. "The baby is peacefully asleep."

"I knew I should've barred him entry," Velom states with a curse. "Nothing good can come from that cowardly male. He should be put down like a crazed animal. He made her cry. I don't understand how, but he did."

"Can we lock him in the brig? For her safety?" Telin asks as he pulls a blanket over her still form. She tries to keep her eyes open, but the drugs are making it impossible.

"I'll talk to Mavito," Velom says. She hears someone sit in the chair, probably Telin. He'll stay there until she wakes up. Then one of the caregivers will force food on her, and maybe, if she begs, let her walk the corridors of the ship with a dozen guards and escorts.

This is her life now. It's all about her safety and well-being and has nothing to do with her actual wishes.

Tears slide down the side of her face as she succumbs to the drugs in her system.

Several days later, Deena is staring down at a plate of food with no interest in eating whatsoever. The portions they give her to eat are huge, and even if she had an appetite, she wouldn't be able to finish them.

She tried putting the food into the room's trash receptacle a few times, but Hirin figured out what she was doing within two meals. She needs to send a message to Mender Dimon so he can intercede on her behalf. She's tired of being dragged to medical to be force-fed nutrient rich liquids just because she doesn't feel like eating or can't finish a plate full of food.

Sitting back, she pushes the plate away and tries to concentrate on ways to mitigate the draconian care of the Hissa in charge of her. She's contacted Lara and Mara repeatedly and both women assured her they're doing their best to bring her concerns before the Council, but it's a slow process hampered by the fact that she doesn't have a mate. Tiran told her bluntly in the last communication that if she would just pick a mate and enter into a Family Pact, she'd automatically have more freedom.

But would she? There's no guarantee that picking a mate would grant her any more freedom than she has already. It would just reduce the number of males who could force her to do things down to one, instead of two dozen.

She contemplates Tiran's words. One male might be easier to get around. Easier to talk into letting her do things. Easier to escape from.

Snorting at that thought, she rolls her eyes. The entire planet of Hissa will be keeping an eye on her now. No escape plan will work once she's back on their homeworld. And because everyone found out that Mara and Tiran helped her, those two won't be let anywhere near her.

Feeling restless, she goes to the cabin door and slaps her hand down on the display to open it. They don't bother locking her in because there're always guards in the hall, so she's allowed that small illusion of privacy. Of course, she can't lock them out either, so it's a poor illusion.

Yopin and Goril are standing guard, and when the door opens, they both swing their gazes to her with identical expressions of concern. "Are you well?" Gorin asks. "Do we need to take you to Medical?"

"Yes to the first, and no to the second," Deena says quickly. "I want to go for a walk. I need to stretch my legs. Can we make that happen?"

Gorin looks like he's going to argue when Yopin steps forward. "We can't take you anywhere near the bay," he warns her. "But the observation deck is at the far end of the ship from here and a nice long walk. Would that be acceptable?"

Last year, when Deena and Lara were first brought to Hissa, one of the guards assigned to them had been a large Hissa warrior named Woken. At the time, Deena thought the guard was as big as a Hissa could get, but Yopin's massive size makes Woken seem average when they stand side by side. If planet continents had voices, they'd sound like Yopin.

"A walk to the observation deck would be great," Deena enthuses. A walk anywhere outside the four walls of her cabin would be a treat. "Aside from the bays, that's my favorite place on the ship."

"We should contact Velom," Gorin protests, and Yopin turns to face the other guard.

"Are you questioning my ability to keep Deena safe?" he asks in a conversational tone that isn't fooling anyone. Gorin looks annoyed. Yopin has a reputation for being quiet and unfriendly. The stories she's heard of him going full berserker during a particularly bad battle lends to his reputation for being antisocial, although she's not sure how the two are related. But she's been warned on numerous occasions that although Yopin isn't dangerous to her, he's not friendly either.

So far, he's been quiet, but affable with no hint of the standoffish attitude she was warned about. But in this situation, his reputation is a boon because Gorin backs down without further protest.

"Fine," he snaps. "We'll go for a walk."

Going to the display in the wall next to her cabin door, he taps a few things and then turns back to them. Smiling up at Yopin, she steps out of her cabin. With a curt nod, Gorin turns and starts moving at a sedate pace down the hall, back rigid and hands locked on his weapon. She can hear Yopin's massive feet hitting the deck plating behind her as they walk. If she looked back, she'd see his head barely clearing the high ceiling of the corridor. When they get to hatches, he has to bend over to go through.

By the time they reach the observation deck, Deena is feeling more relaxed. The ship is on third shift, which is the busiest shift so most of the crew are at their posts and not moving through the halls or hanging out for drinks. The observation deck acts as an informal gathering place, and during first shift, when the least number of crew are working, the place is full of males drinking, gambling, and talking.

She managed to convince the males assigned as caregivers that she needs more interaction, so she's visited the observation deck several times under double the normal guards.

Velom tried to put a stop to it, but Mender Dimon came down on her side, pointing out that isolation would do more harm than good. She's even gotten a taste for one of the Hissa games. Because of the guards, she's not mobbed and those playing the game with her tend to be focused on strategy instead of wooing her. It's enjoyable and refreshing.

The observation deck is empty when they walk in, and Deena can tell by the way Gorin turns to leave immediately that he doesn't expect her to want to remain. But she's not ready to leave. Even if there's no companionship to be found, the observation deck boasts an entire wall of windows and darkened interior. Rows of padded seats face the wall of windows and Deena wants to sit in one and watch the stars. She squares her shoulders, preparing to argue with Gorin so she can stay for a little while. Then Yopin steps in front of her and addresses the other guard.

"I think Deena might be parched from our journey," he rumbles out. "She should sit, and I'll fetch her a drink. There's fresh Soca juice in the galley and I know it's her favorite."

"I'll get it," Gorin says eagerly. He looks over to Deena, his face happy for the first time since they started the walk. "If you would sit and rest, I'll fetch the drink for you. I didn't know Soca was your favorite. I'll make sure we include it with your meals." He hurries off, delighted to provide her with something she wants and maybe earn a smile. Gorin might be all frowns and gloomy attitude with the other Hissa, but he jumps at the chance to earn her favor.

Deena gives Gorin a little smile. "That would be nice, thank you, Gorin."

The guard hurries away, and Deena turns to Yopin, craning her neck to look up at the giant. "You're quiet but manipulative," she murmurs and sees a brief grin cross the behemoth's face. "I like it."

She moves to sit in one of the chairs, expecting Yopin to remain standing and loom over her. Instead, he drops down to sit on the ground next to her. This position puts his face at the same height as hers and makes her feel a lot less crowded. They both stare at the stars in silence for a few moments before Yopin starts talking.

"My mother was fierce and beautiful," he states. Thrown by the non-sequitur, Deena glances over at him, but his attention is still focused on the windows.

"I didn't have a mother," she blurts out.

"I know."

"Right, of course, you know that," she mutters. It was a dumb thing to say. Being Decanted automatically means she didn't have a mother or father. She's just an abomination grown in a vat.

"My mother would like you," he continues. "She was a warrior with a spine of steel."

"She sounds great," Deena comments lamely, unsure what else to say.

"My father told me that when she was pregnant, she kept training until the week before I was born. Even though he asked her to rest, she refused. She said having a child in her only made her stronger and more determined. You're like her." He gestures over his shoulder in the direction Gorin went. "They all think the baby in your belly makes you weak, but it only makes you more resolute."

That's the most she's heard the guard say at once. She's pretty sure that's the most anyone has ever heard him say at one time. His words make her consider picking him for a mate.

If she entered into a Family Pact with him, he could intimidate the hell out of anyone who tried to make her do anything she didn't want to. And by the sound of it, he's not happy with her treatment. But then again, he's never objected to anything Velom and the others have done to her. This walk is the first time he's shown her any kind of overt sympathy.

"Thanks, Yopin," she says, feeling her emotions swirling around in her head, much too confused to bother dissecting or deciphering them at the moment.

"I thought you should know that I see you," he explains simply. "I see you for who you are, not what you are."

"Well," she says with a tired sigh. "You're probably the only one, outside of the other Decanted women."

"No," he counters just as Gorin enters at the far end of the vast room with a glass of juice. "Kilan sees you too."

"Maybe," she hedges.

"And you should know, Mavito isn't happy with how your care is being administered."

That's news to her. "He isn't?"

Yopin leisurely turns his head to regard her. "He knows you have an active mind. That's why he allowed you to have your freedom and kept the crew from finding out you were at the station until after we left. I suspect he knew you were pregnant even then."

"No, he had no idea," she lies quickly, fearful Mavito will get in trouble. Yopin flashes his teeth in a quick smile. Good god, his canines are the length of one of her fingers.

"Don't fib," he says simply.

"Right, well," she flounders. "I guess I'm glad Mavito feels bad for me."

"He sympathizes but is bound by strict adherence to Council dictate and his own duty," Yopin murmurs. "But not all of us are so bound."

That vague statement makes her want to question him further, but the presence of the other guard returning effectively ends their conversation.

"Here it is!" Gorin announces cheerfully, shoving a

canister of liquid at her. She takes it and chokes down the juice she's never tasted before. It's not bad, but not something she'd normally seek out. It's a good thing it's at least palatable because now she's going to be getting it every meal. Oh well, it's a small price to pay.

Gorin tries to make conversation with her, but Yopin puts a stop to it by saying Deena wanted to meditate as she watches the stars. Bless the colossal Hissa warrior and his manipulative ways.

Gorin goes silent and the three of them gaze out at the stars until Gorin makes a noise about taking her back to her room.

The time spent outside her cabin doesn't make it any easier to go back inside the confines of her room, but she passively goes back and picks at the meal still waiting for her.

Perhaps it's time to stop feeling sorry for herself and be more like Yopin's mom. Time to remember how to kick butt. Or, more accurately in her situation, get sneaky.

CHAPTER

17

She hears a few muffled sounds in the hall and wonders if it's time for one of the med techs to scan her again or maybe one of the caregivers is here to check on the progress of her meal.

The last thing Deena expects to see when the door to her cabin opens without warning is Kilan standing there without an escort. The sight is so shocking that she doesn't move when he hurries forward and pulls her to her feet.

She's just about to form words into questions when the sight of three males, unconscious on the floor in the hallway outside her door, shocks her into further silence. It's not until he's shoving her into a small storage locker on a hover cart that she manages to protest.

"What do you think you're doing?" she squawks as he tries to squish her into the tiny space. The hover cart is loaded down with supplies and baggage, leaving only the locker in the very back of the of it empty.

"I already told you," he whispers impatiently, "I'm getting you out of here. I won't stand by and let them treat you like this. But you need to hide in here so I can get you on my ship."

"You have a ship?" she whispers back as she wiggles herself into the cramped space.

"Mavito had a crew go back for it when the fighting was over at the station," he explains with an impatient huff. "It was mostly intact, and he had it repaired by the end of day two of my coma. He said he thought I should have the ability to leave the Steadfast if his crew became too aggressive toward me."

It doesn't even occur to her to fight Kilan as he helps her squeeze into the locker. If he's going to break her out, she's not going to waste time arguing or examining his motives. But there's always room for sarcasm.

"Wasn't that nice of him," she mutters. "Letting you have an escape route in case the guys want to beat you up. Too bad he's only the Commander of the whole damn ship and can't just order his men to stay away from you."

"You're correct. The order wouldn't have been heeded. It was excellent planning on Mavito's part to get my ship," Kilan agrees, either ignoring or missing her tone. He tucks her hands in next to her chest. "I'm going to close the door, but I won't latch it. Try very hard not to move. I'm going to have to get this thing on board quickly and launch. We have a very tight timeline for escape."

"Right," Deena nods and closes her eyes as Kilan shuts her into the tiny space. If she was even a little further along in her pregnancy, there's no way the door would have closed. She feels the cart start to move. She can hear the sound of others talking as they progress, things being moved around, doors opening and closing.

She expects to hear someone shout out at any moment, or the sound of a klaxon going off to tell the crew she's escaped. But no one raises an alarm as they make steady progress. Occasionally, she hears someone shout an insult to Kilan, but he just ignores them.

When the unmistakable smell of the flight deck hits her nose, she smiles despite the knot of nerves in her belly. Soon, she feels the pitch of the cart change as it climbs up a short ramp. There's a pause, then the cart squats down and she hears the latching mechanism of the floor "grab" the bottom of the cart, securing it and its load to the ship.

"Stay hidden for just a bit longer," Kilan whispers through the closed locker door. "I'll launch, and then release you as soon as it's safe."

"Sure," Deena whispers back and contemplates how much she's come to hate the word safe. All manner of liberties have been taken away from her on the pretext of keeping her "safe."

The ship's engines fire up and soon she feels the vibration of a ship underway. Kilan must be pushing the engines hard because it's not much longer before he's opening up the locker and helping her wiggle back out.

"Damn, Kilan," she mutters as she rubs a few sore spots on her body where the unforgiving metal dug into soft flesh. "You don't do anything in half measures. You promised I'd fly again, and then not four days later you're stealing me away."

"Are you hurt anywhere?" he asks anxiously as she carefully straightens her body and absently rubs her belly. She checks in with herself for any worrisome pain or discomfort and shakes her head.

"I'm good," she assures him as she examines the ship with a critical eye. "Is this a Gerina Mark II?" Kilan nods and she gives a little whoop of happiness. "I get to fly next," she declares, pushing him aside so she can cross the cabin and climb into the pilot seat. She hears Kilan chuckle as he settles into the seat next to hers.

Although she's sure they should probably engage in some kind of deep, meaningful conversation about the pregnancy, the Hissa Council, and her abduction/jail break, all she can focus on is the shiny instrument panel in front of her.

"Are those Digon Telemetric displays?" she asks. Kilan nods and she giggles with delight. She leans in a little closer. "Oh, and it's all made of Dimmerion components!" she crows, stroking a panel.

"I wish I was that console," Kilan mutters, and she looks over to see his gaze focused on her hand. She gives the panel a little pat of affection.

"For the male who not only got me off the Steadfast but put me in the pilot seat of a Gerina Mark II," she tells him with a grin, "I might consider some petting and fondling a reasonable request."

His mood shifts at her words. "I didn't do all of this to gain your favor," he answers with familiar sullenness. Deena laughs, making him look up at her with mild surprise.

"You don't do anything to gain my favor," she retorts. "Ever. So, put away the attitude, and let me decide if I want to pet you because I'm happy. Not to mention, I might enjoy touching you.”

With a thoughtful expression, he leans back in his seat and points to the star chart holo-display. “We need to be in that asteroid belt before they know you’re gone,” he comments. “And if you want to touch me, I wouldn’t be opposed.”

It’s a joy to interact with a much less churlish Kilan. Deena checks the chart against the Telemetric display and pulls up a few navigation stats. “That means we have about twenty minutes of travel time before we’re in the clear,” she states and gives him a cheeky grin. “Just so you know, I like to touch naked bodies the best.”

They continue the banter as the minutes tick by and the asteroid belt gets closer. She notices a massive number of ships launching from the Steadfast just as they slip into the dense asteroid belt. She can’t count them, but if it’s near the number the Steadfast is capable of holding, then there are about two thousand fighters heading their way.

“Looks like our grace period is up,” she murmurs and Kilan frowns at the display. He reaches down and inputs a few commands, making the ship around them quake a little, then the engines shut off. The autopilot is shutting down.

“Uh, this seems counterintuitive,” she points out as they start drifting, keeping their original trajectory as the ship moves with residual speed. Kilan holds up a hand to keep her silent as he taps one of the console’s displays a few times. She’s about to start asking questions when a massive ship seems to appear out of nowhere and swallow them up.

Instinctively, she reaches out to take control of the ship and start evasive maneuvers when Kilan’s hand on her arms stops her.

“This is part of the plan,” he assures her.

“Could have warned a girl,” she gripes and sits back in the chair to study the displays around her. She can see they’re in the hull of a giant freighter, surrounded by bits and pieces of broken ships. Bots are jumping from place to place, securing things, breaking apart the wrecks around them for processing, and organizing pieces in different sections. She hears the clang of bots landing on the outside of their ship and startles, hoping this is part of the plan too.

“Telling you wouldn’t have been as entertaining,” Kilan points out, making her laugh.

“I’ll get even,” she warns him.

“You already did,” he replies. “You almost sent me back

into a coma when you told me you were pregnant."

"Ha!" she laughs. "Not sure anyone would have noticed the difference!" He shoots her an unfriendly look, and she chuckles. "So, we hide in this freighter until . . .?"

"This freighter will to launch us in the middle of the Yorlian freight corridor," Kilan explains.

"That's brilliant," Deena compliments him. The Yorlian corridor is one of the busiest in this section of the galaxy. They'll be surrounded by commercial traffic. "What about the transponders?" Kilan rolls his eyes to meet hers and just stares at her with a condescending expression. "Right, you took care of that, I'm sure. What's our identification signature now?"

"We'll register as Fozin," he states, and she winces. "I know, it was all I could get on short notice. The transponders will read genuine and no one, not even the Hissa fleet, will look at us twice. Right now, these bots are on the hull of the ship making it appear older and damaged from micro-meteor strikes. The kind all Fozin end up sporting because of the debris fields near their homeworld."

"Old Fozin ship on the outside," Deena murmurs. "Shiny new Gerina Mark II on the inside. I don't like everyone thinking I'm Fozin, but I have to admit, this is a brilliant plan. What if they notice a random freighter hanging out in the same asteroid belt we disappeared in? Won't they get suspicious?"

"This isn't a random freighter," Kilan tells her. "This belt attracts junk scavengers constantly because so many old ships get caught up with the frozen asteroids." He scans the display in front of him. "Right now, there're about a dozen freighters gathering in this area alone. As we move along, we'll pass hundreds more. The Wayonian own this asteroid and license all the freighters."

"Oh, Wayonian are touchy about that stuff," Deena breathes.

"Exactly. If the Hissa try to search any of these ships to look for us, a call into the Wayonian authorities will be answered immediately. Mavito knows better than to start an intergalactic conflict."

Sitting back, Deena regards Kilan thoughtfully. "You came up with a superb plan," she compliments him. "And on short notice too. It's only been a few days since I saw you last. And what did you do to the guys in the corridor? I didn't hear any struggles."

"I modified a gas bomb with an aerosol of the same drug they gave you the day they dragged me out of the room," he explains, his shoulders tense. "Have they done that often?"

"Drugged me?" she clarifies, and he nods. "All together, they've done that about five times since they brought us on board. The first time was because I lost my shit in med bay. I don't blame them for sedating my ass. I was screaming and fighting them to get to you, and that wasn't helping any of us. But then they started doing it any time I raised a fuss. They probably would've done it to get me away from you while you were healing in med bay, but the ship's primary Mender warned them that dosing me too much might have adverse effects on the baby. So, they only did it when I became 'too upset.'" She sounds a derisive laugh. "No matter what, if I cry, I'm considered 'too upset.' It was hard to keep from crying every time I saw your chest or thought about how close you came to dying. But as long as I didn't cry and didn't fight them scanning me three hundred times a day, they let me stay with you."

"They didn't listen to you," Kilan mutters darkly. "None of them. They didn't listen to you in med bay or later in your cabin. They acted like you weren't even speaking sometimes."

Sighing, she shrugs her shoulders. "It's not the first time I've been treated like that. Hopefully, it'll be the last though."

He nods emphatically. "I'll work very hard to keep you free," he tells her. "I had credits put into a Glonish account, so they won't be able to trace us with purchases, but I won't be able to transfer any more credits so we will need to be frugal."

"Don't worry about that," she assures him. "I'm good at economizing. How much do we have to work with? This thing could take small loads so we can pick up contracts as we travel. Supplementing what we have should be easy."

"I transferred about thirty thousand credits. That's all I could do without raising suspicions."

Deena gapes at him. "Did you say thirty thousand?"

He nods, looking morose. "I wanted to do at least twice that, but it would have taken too long and required much more paperwork. It would have also gotten back to Mavito, and he probably would've put me in the brig on principle."

"Kilan, that's more credits than I could've earned in ten years of steady work," Deena explains. "Don't worry. I can make thirty thousand credits last us for a good long time."

"I'll bow to your knowledge in this area," he says. "But I insist we spend as much as we need on a top-rated medical suite when the baby needs to be born. I refuse to risk your life for any amount of credits."

"I'm not going to argue with that," she agrees with a little shudder. "I'm not so sure about the whole birthing process anyway. I've watched a few vids on human birth, and it looks pretty nasty and painful. I want the med team to give me all the drugs and maybe knock me out. As much as I'm sure I'll love my daughter once she's in my arms, I'm not too interested in the pain she's going to cause getting there."

"Daughter?"

Giving him a brilliant smile, Deena nods. "Yup, daughter."

"May I," he pauses, then shakes himself and turns his attention back to the control console.

"Ask me, Kilan," Deena requests softly. "We're in this together now. I don't expect you to love me, or form a Family Pact with me, or whatever. But I'm willing to take whatever you're willing to give. So, ask me."

Turning to face her, he lowers his eyes to her belly. "May I touch her?"

"There goes my whole twenty-four hours of being tear free," Deena mutters as she turns her chair to face him and scoots herself to the edge of it. She gives a little sniff as she pulls her shirt up to reveal the swell of her pregnancy. "Go ahead, papa. Say hi to your daughter."

Sliding off his chair, Kilan kneels before her, his big hands slowly descending to the bare skin of her stomach, giving her plenty of time to object or recant her permission. She makes no sound of protest as both hands come to rest on her skin. She marvels at how right his touch feels.

"Daughter," he says softly, his entire focus on her belly. "Grow big and strong. I wait eagerly to meet you when you're ready. Don't fear anything. I'll keep you and your mother safe."

Tears roll down her cheeks as Kilan talks to his daughter, and she realizes that for the first time in a long time, the word "safe" doesn't bother her.

CHAPTER

18

After several weeks of travel, Deena finally starts to relax. She's even sleeping full nights now, not waking in a panicked sweat because she dreamed that Mavito found them. When she does have a nightmare, she often wakes up to Kilan holding and talking to her. But he refuses to stay in her bunk. The moment she assures him she feels fine, he goes back to his bed.

She's told him to stay several times, but he always declines. Then she started dropping more hints that she might want to have a physical relationship with him. He's either that clueless or blatantly ignoring her efforts.

He'll flirt with her, but it never goes any further than that, and half the time, the flirting feels half a step away from trading verbal jabs. That's fun too but doesn't help Deena in her pursuit to have sex with Kilan again.

After the last round of flirting, Deena's sure she's going to need to take some extreme measures to get Kilan naked and on top of her. She can't use the excuse of her heat, but maybe she could fake an injury that would require both of them to be naked and in a shower to examine.

Distracted by that thought, she takes a break from scanning contracts for some work at the next station. Looking up, she finds Kilan staring at her and wonders how long he's been doing that. Sitting back, she tilts her head questioningly at him. "What?"

He leans forward slightly with an intense expression on his face. "Who's Gregor?"

She drops her gaze to her hands. "I guess it was too much to hope that you'd forgotten that," she mutters, then looks up. "Are you sure you want to know? You might not like the answer."

Frowning, he regards her with a dark expression. "Was he your owner?"

"Yes and no," she hedges. Kilan makes a sound of impatience, and she holds up a placating hand. "Let me just tell you all of it. That way we get it all out in the open in one painful go instead of drawing it out piecemeal."

Sitting back, she looks down at her belly and gives it an absent-minded rub. "The Addington family is old and powerful," she explains. "They own two entire colonies and several moons. I was told at one point the family numbered in the thousands, but they've shrunk over centuries. Sharil and Harmin were sisters and Sharil had one son. That was the entire Addington clan, three whole people. They were desperate to keep the line going, but Sharil's son wasn't interested in getting married and having kids. He was living the high life on the Galor colony, so Sharil put her foot down. She controlled the family's money and told him he needed to produce an heir, or she'd take extreme measures. She would have too. She thought nothing of punishing people, even if it meant hurting herself in the process." Deena pauses, caught up in the memories of Sharil's cruelty and Gregor's selfishness.

"Was Gregor her son?"

"Yes," Deena takes a shaky breath. "There weren't a lot of single human women on Galor, so first they tried to do a contract marriage, bring a young human woman from Earth all the way out to the colony. After the first few fell apart, Harmin suggested they just buy a wife. That led them to ordering me. And when they did, they had some pretty specific requirements."

Comprehension dawns on Kilan's face. "That's why you go into heat when it's not normal for humans."

Nodding, Deena gives him a small, humorless smile. "Sharil wanted to make sure I'd be a breeder, and if I was ravenous for dick every month, there would be a better chance at having the grandchildren she wanted so badly. That's also why I'm on the short side for a Decanted woman, and my hips are extra wide. Breeding hips. I'm an anomaly among the Decanted women because they had those really specific things they wanted. I'm what they call a 'Special' because I was made-to-order with a trait human women don't normally have."

His face darkens as he asks the next question. "How old were you when they took possession of you?"

"They can age us to six years old in the growing tanks in only six months, so I was Decanted at the biological age of six. After traveling for almost a year to get to Galor, I was about seven when I first met them."

"That's disgusting," Kilan curses, and this time Deena laughs for real.

"Don't worry. They were horrible people, but not that bad. I wasn't touched until I had my first period at fourteen. Until then, life was pretty good. There were tons of servants who were all kind to me. I got lessons in all types of things. It was a pretty good life, considering what happened to a lot of the other Decanted children out there."

"What happened when you were fourteen?"

Blinking back the tears that have been plaguing her since she got pregnant, Deena tries for a nonchalant shrug. "The day after my first period, Gregor and I were married in a quick civil ceremony. It didn't occur to me to protest. I'd been told over and over again that marrying Gregor and having kids was my sole purpose in life. I was looking forward to it. I was young and naïve, and I thought this would make him and Sharil finally love me. I thought we'd be a real family like I saw in all the entertainment vids. I was such an idiot."

"Not an idiot," Kilan counters. "You were young and hopeful."

"I feel like hopeful is just another way to say naïve. Anyway, we didn't consummate the marriage right away. I didn't know what Gregor was waiting for. I'd had sex education at that point. I knew we were supposed to sleep together. I was hurt and confused. Then a few weeks after our marriage, I went into my first heat. I didn't know what was happening, I thought I was sick. Sharil didn't explain anything to me, and my sex education hadn't covered this. Sharil just dragged me into Gregor's room and threw me at him. He started yelling at her, but I don't remember what was said. By the time he collected me from where I collapsed on the floor, I was in a lot of pain." She looks down at her clenched fists and falls silent, fighting back tears. After a few moments, Kilan's big hands close around hers.

"What happened?" he asks in a gentle voice that seems to help her keep the tears at bay.

"I don't remember much," she admits. "At least from that first time. I remember it was fast and it hurt, and then it was over, and I felt better. He left after he was done, told me to stay on the bed. But you know how it goes, the heat isn't over after just one bout of sex. I tried to leave the room when it got painful again, but the door was locked. I screamed for someone to help me, but no one came."

The hands let go of hers and large arms wrap around her and lift. Without a word, Kilan sets her on his lap and tucks her against his chest. She relaxes into him, taking a few deep breaths before she continues. He doesn't need to encourage her to keep talking. Now she wants to tell her story.

"That turned out to be the pattern. My heat would start. He'd have sex with me once, then leave and tell the servants not to let me out of the room for a few days. That was my life from the age of fourteen until twenty-three. I never got pregnant. Sharil had them do all kinds of tests on me, but I didn't find out until I was almost ready to escape that she didn't know her son was only having sex with me once and then leaving me alone for the rest of my heat."

"Is that why you thought you couldn't get pregnant?" Kilan asks, rubbing one of his big hands up and down her back.

"Sharil said that all Gregor's tests came back normal so the problem must be with me. She was so angry because they wasted so much time and money on me, and I was failing at the one thing I was supposed to do. Even after the doctors told her I was healthy and should easily get pregnant, it was still all my fault. For a few years, I tried so hard to get Gregor to stay with me. Begged him to try harder to get me pregnant."

"When did that change?"

"The day he slapped me," she explains, and then gives a little squeak when Kilan hugs her too tightly.

"He hit you?"

"Not very hard," she admits. "I was clutching at him, trying to keep him in the room, and he slapped me a few times to get me to let go and stop begging. He was disgusted, and then he called one of the servants in and told him to fuck me. That's when I realized that while Sharil was obsessed with getting an heir,

Gregor couldn't be bothered to care about anything but his interests."

"I don't understand," Kilan admits, and she pulls her head back enough to be able to see his face.

"What don't you understand?"

"How he could not want you," he says, running a hand up and down her back. "You're so beautiful, and your smell is the most enticing thing I've ever known. How could he have left you over and over again?"

"He liked men," she explains.

Understanding fills his face. "But Sharil needed legitimate heirs, so he couldn't take a male as a partner."

"Exactly. I don't understand why they didn't just send his DNA to the place that produced me and have them create an heir, but my guess is that Sharil didn't think that was acceptable. She made a lot of comments about how her grandchild was going to be half-abomination, but at least it would be biddable, like me." With a little sigh, Deena snuggled her face against this chest. "I'd have felt bad for Gregor, except he was such a bastard. I don't think he would have picked a partner, male or female, to marry unless his mother forced him. He just wanted to have fun."

Shifting a little, Kilan manages to draw her legs around so she's straddling his lap. The new position puts her back to his chest, allowing him to rest one of his big hands on her pregnant stomach. She notices he does that a lot, resting his hand on their daughter. Deena finds it endearing, as long as she doesn't have a full bladder.

"What happened when you were twenty-three?"

"I ran away," she says simply. "I'd been thinking about doing it for a while, and after he told a servant to have sex with me, so I'd stop whining, I finally realized it was never going to get better. If anything, it was only going to get worse. Sharil let me do just about anything I wanted to in my down time so long as I fulfilled all my social and educational obligations, so I took up flying. My instructor told me I was good enough to be employed as a pilot, so once I graduated, I just packed a bag and left. They didn't officially own me as a slave because slaves can't marry or have free children. That means there was no way they could stop me once I was off-planet. I bought a ticket to the nearest station, sent the request for divorce paperwork back to the colony, and looked for work."

"And you got a job as a pilot," Kilan says with pride, and

Deena laughs.

"Not exactly. I was young, didn't have much experience, and didn't know anyone. I worked on a lot of decrepit freighters and cheap passenger transports, filling in as pilot when there was no one else. It took a while, but I finally earned a reputation and managed to get myself a decent paying job. Then I met Lara, and I knew she would need the safety of a ship of our own, so I bought Ally. The ship wasn't great, but it was home for a lot of years."

"That was the same ship that was destroyed during the Raider attack?" Kilan clarifies.

"Yup, poor old ship. It was ancient for a hauler but solid. Anyway, that's the story. Gregor was both my owner and my husband, but never my love, and this little bundle—" She pats her pregnant stomach, her hand coming to rest right next to his. "Is going to get all the love I can possibly give her."

"All that we can give her," Kilan corrects, and Deena feels her heart melt.

"Are you sure about that? You seemed pretty adamant that you didn't want me after the mating marks appeared."

"It wasn't that I didn't want you," he says, kissing the side of her neck. "It was that I knew I'd never be worthy of you."

"Does this have anything to do with Tarim?" The way his body goes stiff and tense is answer in itself, but she presses anyway. "Mavito mentioned that you were going to enter into a Family Pact with a female named Tarim, but she succumbed to the Great Death first."

"Yes," Kilan bites out and then grasps her chin and turns her head. She doesn't fight his grip, expecting that he wants to look into her eyes when he tells her to mind her own business. Instead, she finds herself engaged in a bone melting kiss.

"Let me taste you again," he begs. "We can talk of her later, but I need to put my mouth on you now. I've been careful and chaste with you for the last few weeks, but I find I need you more than my next breath."

His words make her lose her train of thought. All she can do is nod and then gasp when his hands come up to cup her breasts through her biosuit.

"I missed the feel of you so much," he murmurs in her ear. "You were in my dreams every night, and I swear when I woke, sometimes I could almost taste you on my lips."

"I guess I won't need to fake an injury," she murmurs.

"What?"

"Nothing," she tells him quickly. "I want you too. I've been wanting you since the first day I met you. I never stopped wanting you. Even when I was fighting the urge to clobber you with a gear transition cover."

"And I wanted you the moment I met you, even if I also wanted to dump you in a lake to wipe that smirk off your face. You've always tested my control," he groans and stands up, cradling her to his chest. It's a short walk to his larger bunk in the rear of the cabin. Setting her down, he strips off her biosuit with swift efficiency. She notices his hands are shaking slightly and feels her heart swell. She grabs his hands and brings them to her mouth, kissing the back of them.

"The time in the jungle was the best heat I've ever had," she admits to him. "No one ever cared for me like that. No one was ever so gentle and then rough when I needed it. Only you made my heat feel wonderful instead of painful. I might not be in heat now, but that doesn't mean I don't want you any less."

Suddenly, Kilan isn't gentle anymore. With a grip just shy of painful, he pulls her legs apart and practically dives for her sex. Unprepared for the assault, Deena cries out, first in surprise, and then in pleasure as his mouth works on her. When his hands reach up and palm her breasts, kneading the flesh and plucking at her nipples, she groans and twists under him.

"I guess you remember what I like," she pants.

Bringing his face up for a moment he looks at her with a mixture of adoration and intense focus. "Every part of our time in the jungle is etched in my memory like carvings on a stone. Every time you made a sound, every word you spoke, every movement I hoarded like a man starved. I treasured every precious memory. I never thought I'd be allowed to touch you again."

"That's sweet," she coos, and then urges his head back down. "But I'm not interested in talking at the moment." He chuckles, his breath fanning out on her skin. She's about to make another sardonic comment, but he starts licking and sucking again.

"You're good at that," she moans, writhing under him. It doesn't take long for her orgasm to wash over her, making her bow against him and cry out. He doesn't stop until she tries to jerk away from him. He lifts himself until he's kneeling between her legs so he can remove his shirt. It's then that she notices he's not wearing pants anymore. Engorged and beautiful, his cock juts out proudly, and she sits up a little to reach for it. He grabs her searching hand with one of his and urges her to lie back down.

"I won't last if you touch me," he tells her, his voice tight and his expression pained. "I want to be inside you again. I need to feel you surrounding me. Tell me this is acceptable," he begs.

Mutely, she nods and lets herself fall back on the bed as he uncoils his body over hers. She widens her legs to accommodate his hips and gives a little sigh of contentment when she feels the head of his erection nudging the folds of her sex. She's braced for him to ram himself inside of her, but instead, he eases his way. There are no jolts of discomfort or pain, only a pleasant stretching that soon turns to a lovely sensation of being full. When his pelvis bumps hers and rubs deliciously on her still sensitive clit, she wonders if it's possible for her to climax like this even though she's not in heat.

"More," she demands, wrapping her legs around him.

"No," he starts to say, moving slowly to withdraw from her and worried he's going to stop the whole process, she tightens her legs and thrusts her hips up. The move pushes him hard into her, making them both gasp.

"I want you to enjoy it," he tells her.

"I am," she promises.

"I don't want to hurt our daughter."

She shakes her head. "You won't. I talked to Dimon. Sex is safe."

In truth, Mender Dimon said she could resume all normal physical activities within reason, but he hadn't said anything specifically about sex. Sex seems like a pretty normal activity, though, so she's sure she's not lying. Besides, stopping now isn't an option.

"Let me," he begins to say and before he can finish his statement, Deena rears up and grabs him by the neck, clinging to him with her arms and legs. With frantic need, she tries to move so she can get the wonderful sensations again. She makes a frustrated sound when she can't get the angle right, and Kilan lowers them both to the bed.

"Easy," he murmurs soothingly, even as his breathing is getting ragged with need. "Lie back. Let me do the work."

"Now!" she insists. She can feel a second orgasm looming and might need to murder the bastard if he doesn't start moving soon.

Supporting his weight on his elbows and knees, he starts thrusting. Slowly at first, then building to a rhythm that makes her moan and clutch at him. He keeps his face close to hers, kissing her and whispering words to her that she can't be bothered to understand.

When she feels the second orgasm start to move through her, she screams his name, tightening her body down and making him cry out with pleasure. He follows her, thrusting a few more times as he finds his release: then he drops to the bed, rolling her on her side so they can remain intertwined as the aftershocks of their pleasure roll through them.

"So that's what it feels like," she murmurs.

"What are you referring to?" he asks, running gentle fingers through her hair and laying a few kisses on her cheek.

"Sex without the heat," she explains. "I always wondered what it would be like but never bothered to try." His body tenses against hers.

"Was it . . . Did you . . .?" he fumbles a few words out and then stops, his voice hesitant and anxious.

She opens her eyes just enough to see his apprehension and give him a languid smile. "Can't wait to do it again." His expression is one of both relief and pleasure.

"Thank you," he whispers, drawing her body tightly against his own.

"Sure thing," she says with a yawn. "And later, it'll be your turn to tell me about Tarim, considering I told you all about my painful past."

Instead of tensing up and pulling away from her, he nuzzles her cheek. "I'm afraid to tell you."

She doesn't open her eyes. "Why?"

"Because you'll realize I'm not worthy."

Huffing out a laugh, she wiggles a little so she can throw an arm over him and nestle her face against his chest. "I already knew that. But I'll let you work on being worthy. It might take a few decades, but we'll get you there." Another yawn splits her face, and she's already asleep before Kilan can think of a response.

CHAPTER

19

"I don't like this," Kilan grumbles.

"I heard you the first five times," she counters without stopping. While the baby bump isn't making her horribly awkward yet, she does find that she moves much slower now than she used to. Thankfully, Halm station isn't very busy today, so she doesn't need to navigate any crowded thoroughfares. Kilan keeps glaring at anyone who gets close to her, so that helps also. She just wishes he'd stop complaining about the danger of visiting the station.

In truth, staying on the ship would be wiser, but she's always wanted to see Halm's famous Star Dome, so remaining onboard ship while the ship is being fueled and serviced isn't an option.

"By repeating it, I hope you'll eventually realize how dangerous this is and return to the ship," Kilan shoots back. She's never going to admit it to him, but she likes his no-holds-barred grumpiness. All the other Hissa were always on their best behavior with her, most never showing a hint of their real personality, but not Kilan. He was brusque and surly with her from day one, and she wouldn't trade his attitude for the world.

"Fuss all you want," she taunts him. "It's not going to change my mind. I read that there's a restaurant just under the center of the dome. I think I might need to eat there now." His sound of annoyance makes her chuckle.

"You enjoy being contrary," he accuses.

"Maybe," she agrees with a grin. Whatever he's about to retort is lost on her because they've just passed through an arch into the center of the station. The sight that greets her eyes takes her breath away, and she comes to a complete standstill, much too busy taking everything in to move.

She vaguely hears a few annoyed protests because she's partially blocking the arched entryway, but she ignores them. Kilan comes up behind her and wraps his big arms around her, making the moment perfect.

Pictures and vids of the Star Dome are nothing compared to actually seeing it. The massive stained-glass dome stretches out over a large circle of shops and restaurants on the multi-tiered market area. Unlike most stations, Halm circles a sun instead of a planet, and the orbital engines keep the station turned toward the sun so bright light shine through the glass, casting swatches of color on the floor and walls of the area. The complex geometric pattern shifts constantly as the glass panels move in undulating forms, powered by small solar cells embedded in the metal frames of each panel. The nearby sun's solar flares and coronal ejections are what influence the fluctuating dome's luminescence. Because the whole thing moves according to the sun, the patterns can be unpredictable. Harsh one moment and fluid the next.

Right now, the dome is moving with lazy, sluggish twirls, making the colored light pattern below flow like slow-moving ripples in a pond. Deena has an almost overwhelming urge to lie down in the center so the colored light can move over her. Shaking herself out of the fantasy, she looks up to Kilan, expecting to see him as transfixed by the amazing sight as she was, only to find he was staring at her the entire time.

"You're beautiful," he tells her softly. "Everyone else is too busy to bother admiring what is right in front of them, except you. Despite all the things you've experienced, you're willing to brave capture to experience something of beauty but not practicality."

"Practicality can only get us so far," she murmurs back. "We still need to feed our souls with other things."

"What of the heart?"

"That needs to be given a diet of love and loyalty," she tells him. "Just like you feed me."

"I'm lucky," he whispers to her. "Everyone here only gets to view this kind of beauty while they walk the station. But I get to hold it in my arms every night." He leans down to kiss her, and she eagerly stretches up to meet his lips.

"I think someone's been reading up on human romance etiquette," she pants after they draw back from the kiss.

"Would human romance etiquette include a meal under the dome?" Kilan asks as he leads her to the small restaurant she mentioned earlier.

"It absolutely would," she agrees and sits at the table he picks. They both study the display on the table and make a few selections. Deena winces at the cost of even the basic items but decides not to say anything. Kilan isn't romantic often. She might as well enjoy it.

"I apologize for my bad mood," he says after they've finished ordering. "I know the danger here is minimal, but I find I'm rather irrational when it comes to you."

Deena laughs. "You and every other Hissa."

Scowling at her observation, he grabs one of her hands in his. "I don't find that a flattering comparison."

Returning his grip, she smirks. "It wasn't meant to be. But if it makes you feel better, you're one of only two Hissa in the universe who listens to me. That means a lot in my book."

"Who's the other?" he growls out.

"Mender Dimon," she says with a chuckle. "Don't worry. I'm not interested in him. Besides, I believe it's your daughter I'm carrying around, so I think the jealousy is a little unnecessary."

Taking a deep breath, Kilan manages to stop scowling at her. "And now I must apologize again."

Deena uses her free hand to pat his forearm. "Don't worry about it. I'm not fragile. Your grumpiness isn't going to send me running. If it gets really bad, I'll just find some way to distract you," she tells him with a suggestive lilt to her voice.

They trade gentle barbs and chat about inconsequential things as they wait for their food. Deena finds herself getting overheated and curses the pregnancy. It seems having a child growing in her belly means her body's heating and cooling systems are all out of whack. Right now, she's starting to sweat, even though she knows the actual temperature on the station hasn't changed. Desperate to cool down even a little bit, she undoes the collar of her biosuit and opens up the top a few inches, drawing back the edges so her damp skin can get a little air.

A strangled sound draws her attention to Kilan, who's staring at her neck. He's gone pale, and his eyes are wide again. The hand holding hers tightens and all thoughts of being overheated vanish.

"Kilan?"

He shakes his head as if coming out of a dream and raises his gaze to meet her eyes. "I'm sorry. I knew they'd reappear. I just wasn't ready for them."

It takes Deena a moment to realize what he's talking about, and then she brings her hand up to her neck, self-consciously rubbing the skin there. She can't see them, but she knows the mating marks must be back.

"I wouldn't trade them for anything," she tells him. "I'm glad they're there. I want them there."

"You hid them before. I was told you kept them hidden from sight until they were gone." He doesn't sound accusatory, just wary. It's strange to see her strong, confident Kilan looking uneasy, even vulnerable.

"I didn't want to be stared at," she explains. "All the guys were already looking for any excuse to talk to me or touch me. Because everyone knew you weren't in the picture, all the mating marks would have done was make me more desirable. Every single guy who saw them would just picture his mating marks on me. I felt too raw to handle that."

"I caused you so much pain," Kilan says softly.

"You did," she agrees but holds tightly to his hand when he tries to draw away. "But I'm damn sure you were hurting too."

Nodding, Kilan stops trying to remove his hand and grasps her back. "Her name was Tarim, and she was stunning."

Ignoring the spike of jealousy that his words cause, Deena nods her head. "Tell me more."

"She wasn't anything like you," he says, closing his eyes for a moment as if picturing Tarim in his mind. "She was shy, soft-spoken, and delicate. She liked fine clothes and perfumes. I remember begging my parents for credits so I could buy her things. Her face would light up, no matter how small the gift. She always told me that just being given something to open was as important as the actual content of the gift itself. I wanted to give her things so badly that I wrapped up a box of flowers I picked from a nearby jungle path. When she opened the box, she acted like I'd given her precious jewels."

Deena wants to hate the dead woman, but Kilan's words are so full of love and remembered happiness that all she can feel is pain for his loss. "She sounds amazing."

Opening his eyes, Kilan gives her a small, wan smile. "We were very young, but I knew. I just knew we were meant to be mates. Both our parents seemed to know too. They didn't try and limit us. Although it's uncommon, we had a Knowledge Period young, and she developed mating marks even though we hadn't reached the full age of maturity." She touches the marks on her neck, not realizing she's doing it until his eyes come to rest there. He reaches out and draws her hand away. and then uses one blunt finger to trace part of the pattern.

"Her pattern was bright, like yours," he murmurs. "But not so tightly woven." He takes a deep breath and sits back, still keeping a hold of her hand. "We were going to enter into a Family Pact, but both our parents wanted us to wait until we'd picked careers. Even before the Great Death, our species population wasn't as numerous as others. Before we had children, they wanted both of us to train and work for several years. We agreed, but we just couldn't stay away from each other. Our parents didn't try very hard to temper our behavior, so it wasn't a surprise to anyone when she became pregnant."

Jolting at the news, Deena's eyes go wide. "Pregnant?" she whispers, horrified. No emotion shows on Kilan's face when he nods.

"That's when the Great Death hit. My mother succumbed first, then her sister, and her mother. Finally, she got sick." Hissa aren't physiologically capable of crying, so Deena lets the tears roll down her face for both of them.

"Tell me," she requests softly. He brings a hand up to wipe the tears away. "Don't worry about that," she says as she grabs his hand in her own so now both of his hands are clutched tightly in hers. "Finish it."

"She was in so much pain." His voice is so quiet she has to lean forward to hear him. "By the time she got sick, the disease had killed so many. No cure. No way to stop it. I knew what was going to happen. Her family knew too. They let me stay with her. I talked to her. Talked to our child. I told them everything would be fine. I lied and lied. I told them I'd take them to the stars. I'd show them red suns and blue planets. Soon she couldn't hear my words because her pain was too great."

A delivery bot arrives and sets their food on the table, but neither of them reaches for it. Deena grasps his hands so tightly that her fingers ache. She's glad to know what happened but feels sick to cause Kilan so much pain by bringing up horrible memories.

"She was in such agony," he tells her, his face twisting into an expression of horror as he loses himself in the memory. "She screamed so much she lost her voice. She begged me." He stops talking, but Deena already knows.

"She asked you to kill her. To put an end to the pain."

Letting out a ragged breath, he nods. "It's the last gift she begged me for, to release her from the agony. To send her and our child across the starry veil." She doesn't need him to finish the story. The evidence of what he did is written in pain on his face.

"You did an honorable thing," she tells him, and his gaze slides up to meet hers, stunned. "What you did took courage and love, never think otherwise."

"I was weak," he whispers, shame replacing his stunned expression. "I took her life with my own hands. Her father found me with my hands around her neck. He didn't say a word. He just left the house and walked out into the jungle. No one ever saw him again." Kilan takes several shuddering breaths. "It was all my fault. All of it. What male takes the life of his female and child instead of protecting them?"

"A male who knows that's the only way to end their suffering," she states firmly. "The cowards are those who let their loved ones suffer. You knew there wasn't a cure. There wasn't any way to stop the pain. One of the first things I did when I got to Hissa was to research the Great Death. I know you guys have a vaccine now, but I was a little leery and I wanted to make sure Lara and I weren't getting ourselves into a potential life-ending situation. I found myself watching vids of females sick and dying. Every single one of them begged their loved ones to kill them. To stop the pain. As much as I wish I could go back and unsee those vids, there's one good thing that came out of it. I can tell you that I know with absolute certainty, you did the right thing by Tarim."

They both lapse into silence, Deena because she doesn't know what else to say, and Kilan because he seems to be considering her words. She glances over to the plates of food, but the thought of eating makes her feel ill. So much for their romantic meal under the dome. This just means they'll need to come back and do it again someday. That thought makes her feel mildly better.

"You shouldn't want to be with me anymore," he finally says, and Deena gives into impulse and launches herself awkwardly into his lap. She takes Kilan by surprise, and he grunts as he scrambles to keep her from smacking into the table or tumbling off him. Once situated, she wraps her arms around his neck and hugs him tightly, kissing him several times before pulling back so she can look into his eyes.

"This only makes me want you more," she tells him firmly. "You might as well just chuck the whole self-pity thing out the airlock. You belong to me and the baby. And I can tell you right now, we're never letting you go." The look of utter joy on his face makes her damn eyes start up the waterworks. Sniffing, she buries her face in the crook of his neck.

"You mean that," he says, clearly awestruck. "Even after knowing what I did. What evil I'm capable of, you still want to be with me?"

"I don't just want to be with you," she answers. "I'm pretty sure I love you too, you arrogant jerk. And stop saying you're evil or unworthy or stupid Pienter shit like that. You're annoying and exasperating, but all the other stuff isn't true."

His arms tighten around her, and Kilan heaves out a long breath. "You're a gift I'll never deserve."

"Damn straight," she responds. "But if you let me pilot us around the next gas giant, I might concede you deserve me a little." She feels him chuckle against her. Then she feels his body stiffen, and he takes in a sharp breath. There's not much that would make him react like that. Dread fills her as a familiar voice hits her ears.

"The moons of Hissa lit my path to the two of you, Mater Deena Clanless and Pater Kilan," Mavito addresses them using the formal name for father, but his voice is full of regret. "I wish with all my heart the path had been dark."

CHAPTER

20

"No," Deena moans against Kilan's neck, closing her eyes tightly and willing this to all be a bad dream.

"I'm very sorry I've found you," Mavito says, and Deena looks up to see them surrounded by Hissa soldiers. The expression on Mavito's face is resigned.

"Just turn around," Deena begs. "Pretend you don't see us."

None of the soldiers around them have their helms up, so she can see their facial expressions, ranging from satisfaction to morose. Although the Hissa assigned to her on the Steadfast rarely listened to her, she saw more than one disapproving look from other soldiers at her treatment. Perhaps there are allies here.

"You know I can't do that," Mavito says with real regret.

"Please," she begs, meeting the eyes of the soldiers surrounding them. "Please don't do this. They'll separate us. They'll ground us. Don't take the stars from us."

"Calm yourself," Mavito orders. "If you follow me without fighting, I'll see what I can do to keep you two together. The rest isn't up to me, but for now, I can do that."

"No one touches Deena without her permission," Kilan demands, and Mavito nods.

"I agree unless she's unable to give her consent. In that case, we'll perform all life-saving measures necessary."

Kilan turns his gaze to her. "Is that acceptable? I'm willing to fight if you want me to, but I don't want to risk you getting hurt."

"No fighting," she says firmly and turns her eyes to Mavito. "As long as we're kept together, and no more drugging me just because I'm crying, I won't try to escape."

For some reason that makes Mavito's lips quirk. "Agreed. The males that were in charge of you might be less inclined to drug you now that they've had a taste of their own medicine, so to speak." Several of the soldiers chuckle at his words, and it takes a moment for her to remember how Kilan neutralized her guards.

Slowly standing up, Kilan cradles her to his chest. "I can walk," she reminds him, but he doesn't move to set her on her own feet.

"Can I carry you instead?" he asks. "I find I'm reluctant to let go."

Twining her arms back around his neck, she lets her head drop to his shoulder. "I never want you to let me go," she admits and gives the magnificent dome one last look as the soldiers fall in step around them. She can't seem to stop the tears now, and once the dome is out of sight, she buries her face against Kilan and just lets her eyes leak.

Someday we're going to have a conversation about how you made your mom a teary-eyed mess, she silently tells her daughter. *And hopefully we're going to laugh about it because I'm damn tired of crying.*

Despite Mavito's assurances, Kilan becomes more and more tense as they walk the corridors of the Steadfast. The trip to the dock was uneventful. Most bystanders didn't even give them a second glance. Once on board, all that changes. Every single Hissa they pass stare with wide eyes when they see Deena in his arms. If he has to guess, they're probably surprised because Mavito kept the reason for docking on Halm a secret.

Why would the Section Commander need to keep this

mission a secret? The only answer he can come up with is that not everyone on the Steadfast agrees with going after the two of them. That might prove helpful later. A glance down at Deena shows her studying faces as they pass.

His clever little pilot is aware of the potential for help from sympathizers as well. Even among those Mavito picked to escort them off the station, he saw expressions denoting disgust at the assignment. Mavito couldn't even put together ten team members who believed wholeheartedly in retrieving the wayward couple.

"How'd you find us?" Kilan asks, and Mavito glances back with a slight frown. "You might as well tell us. Deena's given her word we won't attempt to escape."

"We put trackers on your ship," Mavito admits.

"I know," Kilan answers. "I stripped them off before leaving the bay."

"You stripped all but one off before you left the bay," Mavito corrects him. "There was a small one hidden in the bio-recycler."

"That's a good hiding place," Kilan concedes. It never occurred to him to check any of the bio systems. The very nature of the work those systems do would render most tracers inert after only a few minutes of being brought online.

"I had one specially constructed so it could survive," Mavito explains, accurately anticipating Kilan's next question. "When I realized it was the only tracker you didn't find, I tried to track you down without it. I didn't expect you to concoct and execute such an elaborate escape plan so quickly. I should've known better." Mavito gives Kilan an admiring glance. "You eluded us so quickly and effectively that I was taken completely by surprise."

Kilan doesn't respond to Mavito's implied compliment. "With that tracker, we should've been caught within days."

"That particular tracker was only meant to be a last resort. Even with the special casing, it still only worked for a few hours once we activated it. Even then, the signal was weak, and we only had a rough idea of where you were. We were forced to note all the ships in the area and slowly check each one for you. It took us a great deal of time tracing down false leads before we zeroed in on your ship, but you did such an excellent job at disguise that no one could confirm it was you. We didn't want to cause an incident by capturing a Fozin ship, so we followed you until you docked here. Once we visually confirmed it was the two of you, we docked a second shuttle with a team to capture you." A note of admiration creeps into Mavito's voice. "I was very thrown by the ship. It didn't look at all like yours and all the readings came back that it wasn't a Gerina Mark II. How did you change the engine power signatures?"

"I rigged a regulator to randomly throttle engine output," Kilan explains.

Mavito barks out a laugh. "Brilliant. Remind me to recommend to the Council that you be assigned to intelligence gathering."

"I doubt they'll be assigning me anywhere but the incarceration facility on Brimming," Kilan points out dryly and feels Deena stiffen in his arms.

"If they put you in prison, then I'm going too," she declares stubbornly. "And I'll make everyone's life hell the entire time it takes me to get there." Several of their escorts chuckle at her words.

"What's hell?" one of the guards whispers to another one.

"Someplace bad?" the other responds, causing more chuckles.

"Don't make me show you," Deena threatens, making even Mavito smile.

"I hate the circumstances of our reunion," Mavito tells them. "But I'm heartened to find the two of you have formed an accord."

"Accord?" Deena scoffs. "He's mine. No one takes away what's mine."

A few of the guards glance over to Deena, then to Kilan, envy on their faces. It's the goal of every unattached Hissa male to find a Decanted female who will claim them with the same raw fierceness as Deena just claimed him.

Feeling his heart swell with adoration for this female, he uses the brief moment they come to a stop to wait for a corridor to clear to bring his face to hers for a kiss.

"You have my heart," he admits both to her and himself. "I want to be your mate. I want to enter into a Family Pact and have your marks tattooed on my neck. I want it all."

"I knew that," she whispers back.

"How could you? I didn't realize it until now," he retorts gruffly.

"Because only someone who loved me would be willing to take me away from the safety provided by the Hissa homeworld so that I could be free. You went against your people and your instinct. If that's not love, then I don't know what is."

"You're an unapparelled female," he tells her with another kiss.

"I know," she smirks. "Go ahead, you can admit it. I'm a better pilot too." That comment makes all the guards chuckle, and Kilan works to keep a mock scowl on his face.

"You crashed on your first test flight," he points out, and she punches his chest with no real force.

"The shuttle failed, you moron," she says with faux outrage. Their conversation is interrupted when the corridor clears of equipment and a dozen familiar faces appear to block their path. All humor drops away, and Kilan feels Deena's body go stiff in his arms.

"Velom," Mavito greets the guard at the front of the group. Kilan's not sure, but he thinks most of these males in the group blocking their path served as Deena's guards, med techs, and caregivers.

"You should have taken us with you," Velom states, his voice tense, and his expression angry.

"I've reassigned all of you," Mavito reminds them. "None of you should be here at this time. Report to your normal duties. The males I've assigned to Deena are all competent and waiting for her. You're no longer needed for her care."

"At least let me take this one to the brig," a guard next to Velom spits out, pointing to Kilan.

"No," Deena protests, tightening her arms around his neck. "Mavito said we could stay together."

"He shouldn't be near you, Deena," Velom explains, his voice gentle. "He kidnapped you. He could've hurt you. Just remain calm, and we'll get you away from him."

If Kilan hadn't spent the last weeks watching Deena so closely, he wouldn't have known she was fighting not to cry. "Be easy, little pilot," he whispers to her. "Let's see if Mavito can keep his word." Deena nods but doesn't talk.

"I'm in control of this ship," Mavito points out, his voice calm, but his body rigid. "You're under my command, Velom. I'm ordering you to return to your duties and avoid contact with either of them."

Velom smirks and holds out a data pad to Mavito. "The Council isn't happy with you right now. Councilor Damir approved my request for unilateral rights over Deena until we reach homeworld. You might be the commander of this ship, but I don't answer to you any longer, I answer directly to the Council."

With barely suppressed violence, Mavito snatches the data pad from Velom and glances through the transmission displayed there. Kilan holds his breath as Mavito reads, hoping the male has some kind of rebuttal to Velom's claim. But Mavito looks up with an apologetic expression. Before he can even talk, Deena loses her fight and starts quietly crying.

"No," she shakes her head violently. "No, no, no! Mavito, you promised!"

"I'm sorry, Pilot Deena Clanless. My authority over you has been revoked," Mavito tells her with his face full of anguish. "Kilan, you need to put her down. My men will escort you to the brig as the Council has demanded. Velom will be in charge of Deena's care."

"My men will take him," Velom interjects aggressively, and Mavito graces him with a humorless smile.

"This order only states that you're in charge of Deena and that Kilan must be housed in the brig for the remainder of the journey. It gives you no rights to my brig or Kilan. If you wish to contest this, please feel free to forcefully object." Kilan realizes that Mavito is baiting Velom, hoping the other man will cause problems and once again fall under Mavito's authority.

Velom glares at Mavito for a moment but finally nods his head. "Very well, Kilan's yours." Stepping forward, he holds out his arms. "Give her to me," he demands. "She's my primary duty. Locking Kilan in a cell is of much lesser importance. Do as you wish with the unworthy male."

Kilan lowers Deena to her feet instead of handing her to Velom. If he has to fight it's better if he's not holding her. To everyone's shock, Deena launches herself at Velom the moment her feet touch the floor. The guards are so surprised that she's able to grab one of his weapons and withdraws back against Kilan, shielding his larger body with her own.

"Back off," she growls. "Back off or I shoot."

"Put down the weapon," Mavito commands, his voice steady, but there's fear on his face. Kilan looks around at the guards, both Mavito's and Velom's. None of them have drawn any weapons, but all of them have triggered their armor suit's helms. With the armor fully engaged, it would take repeated accurate strikes by the weapon Deena's holding to take even one of them down. They don't plan on firing. They plan on rushing her, absorbing her shots, and physically restraining her.

In a flash, Kilan realizes there's no way they'll be able to leave, not even with Deena holding a weapon and using her smaller body to shield him.

Reaching around her, he plucks the weapon out of her hand and tosses it to Mavito. She swings around, anger and hurt registering on her face. "Why did you do that? I could have saved you."

"Not the right moment," he answers. "Not the right way. They'd be desperate to keep you from leaving, and you might get hurt in a scuffle, even if they don't fire on you. I couldn't risk that."

"I'd rather get hurt than lose you," she argues.

"You haven't lost me yet," he assures her. "We're just going to be separated for a time."

It's obvious from the expression on her face that she doesn't believe him. "Yeah, as if the Council is just going to let us go on living happily ever after."

Kilan doesn't get a chance to say anything further as arms come around Deena and lift her away. Several others grab him and drag him backward. "Don't fight!" he yells at her, but she's too busy writhing and screaming in Velom's grip to hear him. When he sees Manel with the drug gun, he starts fighting the hands restraining him.

"Don't drug her! Take her to a room and let her calm down. Just don't drug her!" His pleas fall on deaf ears as Manel puts the drug gun to her neck, and her body goes limp. Her eyes stay on him as they carry her away, tears streaming down her face.

"Listen to her!" he screams at them. "Velom, Manel, Yopin, everyone, you need to listen to her." He knows it's fruitless, so he stops fighting the hands holding him and turns pleading eyes on Mavito.

"You need to make them listen to her. It's her worst nightmare to have no control. She needs to feel like she has some independence. Please, Mavito, just make them do that."

"I'll try," Mavito says and gestures to the men holding him. "Take him to the brig and post guards. I don't want anyone getting into his cell unless I authorize it."

"This isn't right," Kilan mutters, fighting the violent fear rising in him at the thought of what Deena must be going through. "None of this is honorable."

"When our species is dying, it's hard to act honorably,"

Mavito says grimly and then turns on his heels and strides away.

"Come with me, Kilan," one of the guards tugs at his arm. "We'll try and keep you updated on Deena, but for now you need to come with me."

Numbly, Kilan follows the guards. "If we have to hurt the females who carry our young," he mutters to himself. "Maybe we're a species that doesn't deserve to survive."

CHAPTER

21

Kilan can't seem to calm himself. The guards who put him in the brig were friendly, and even offered to get him an unconnected data pad loaded with entertainment vids or readings of his choice. He refused, knowing there was no way he can sit still to view anything on a data pad. Instead, he spends hours pacing his cell, pausing only long enough to occasionally bang his fist against a wall before resuming his circuit of the room.

At first, the guards asked him to quiet his activities but gave up after he cursed at them. When the main door to the brig opens, he looks up, hoping to see Mavito. He's both disappointed and surprised when it's Laxon who walks into the brig.

The gunner strides over to the front of his cell with a furious expression, and Kilan expects him to start castigating, but instead, he glances over to the guards. "Janin, Somar, can I request a moment of privacy to speak to an old comrade?"

"He's not to be left alone," Somar states slowly, glancing meaningfully over at Janin. "We can't leave the room because you requested it."

"Did you hear that?" Janin asks, canting his head as if listening. Somar gives a little grin and nods.

"I believe I hear something suspicious in the hall also," he agrees. "I know you're not trained for guard duty, Gunner Laxon, but would you be willing to assume the responsibility for a short time while Somar and I make sure there aren't any issues in the hall? It shouldn't take us long."

"I accept reasonability for the detained," Laxon replies with a curt nod.

Kilan hopes he isn't going to need to physically defend himself against his former shipmate. He initially didn't worry about reprisal for kidnapping Deena because Mavito was so adamant that no one could have access to him without permission. But if feelings against him are too strong, Mavito's orders can and will be circumvented.

Turning his attention back to Kilan, Laxon's eyes don't waver as the two guards leave the brig. Kilan waits for Laxon to make the first move. He can easily walk over to the control console at the far end of the room and open Kilan's cell, but the man just stands there, stiff and silent.

"We don't agree with any of this," he finally states. Confusion fills Kilan, but before he can ask any of the dozens of questions that pop into his mind Laxon continues.

"Velom and his group are overstepping. I know they're doing it because they're worried about Pilot Deena Clanless, but everyone knows the best person to give her care is her mate. That's you. But instead of being by her side, you're here locked in a cage. What's happened to us that we separate mates?"

Unsure how to respond, Kilan remains silent and waits. It's obvious the gunner has more to say. Now it's Laxon's turn to pace.

"The incident earlier is all over the ship," Laxon informs him. "Deena demanded to stay with you. She fought to stay with you. They had to drug her to make her stop fighting. In the past, we would've never drugged a Hissa woman. We would never force a mated pair to flee because they couldn't be together. We would never have taken a woman's freedom away from her. The Council doesn't seem to want to listen to reason, especially Councilor Damir. He's obsessed with keeping the Decanted women locked away for their own good. That was never who we were, and it shouldn't be who we are now."

Breathing raggedly from heavy emotions, Laxon rubs his hands over his face, his shoulders slumping a little. When he looks up, his face is twisted with disillusionment. "My sister would be so disappointed in us. She always wanted to be a gunner. I wanted to go into mining but switched to the military after she died. If she couldn't be a gunner, I was going to fulfill her legacy for her." He rubs shaking hands on the back of his head, another show of his agitation.

"She would've fought for you, Kilan. You and your mate," he states adamantly. "She would've fought, so I'm going to fight in her stead."

"I just need to be with Deena," Kilan requests, unsure of what Laxon can accomplish.

In the power structure of the ship, Laxon doesn't command a great deal of authority, but perhaps he and others can intervene on his behalf and help persuade Velom to relax his strict control over Deena. It hasn't been long enough for the drugs to wear off yet, but the moment they do, he knows his Deena will be angry and ready to fight some more. They can't keep drugging her so he fears they might start to physically restrain her. His concern must have shown on his face because Laxon's next words are spoken in a soothing tone.

"There are many on the ship who agree with me," he explains. "Several members of the flight crew were shipped back to homeworld because they objected to going after you. We all saw surveillance videos. Deena willingly went with you. She voluntarily climbed into the storage locker. Despite Velom's vitriol, we know she wants to be with you. Mavito didn't want to chase you down and took as much time as he could before apprehending you two. But Mavito would never go against the Council's orders. The rest of us aren't so sure we want to be loyal anymore."

Laxon's words shock Kilan. After the Great Death, the Hissa were so decimated that those who were left developed a strong sense of community and loyalty, to the point of blind obedience in some cases. It never occurred to him that so many might not only be questioning the Council's decisions, but also be contemplating outright defiance.

"Try to remain calm and ready," Laxon tells him mysteriously.

"Ready for what?"

For the first time since entering the brig, Laxon smiles. "I'm not sure yet," the gunner admits. "But I'm sure my sister will be proud when it happens."

With that ambiguous statement, Laxon turns on his heels

and strides out of the brig. Janin and Somar come back in the moment he's gone and resume their seats, chatting amicably about a game of chance they both play.

Ignoring them, Kilan sits heavily on the hard cell bunk. Stress twists his gut as he realizes that his and Deena's fate are now directly tied into the developing tensions between the Council and most of the men on the Steadfast. There's no way this ends well for everyone, but he hopes at least Deena is given more freedom.

Lying back on the bunk, he closes his eyes and brings forward the memories of Deena standing under the Star Dome. Before they sat to eat, and he shared his past. It's one of the most perfect moments of his life.

He must have drifted off because the sound of struggling wakes him. Sitting up on his bunk, Kilan watches an unfamiliar face flail between two guards as they drag him into the cell next to his. The uniform tells Kilan that his new neighbor is a gunner, like Laxon, but operates on the big guns aboard Steadfast instead of the remote guns mounted on drones. The stench tells him that this man overindulged and probably caused enough problems to be confined for a time.

"Flush yourself out an airlock," a slurred voice shouts out.

"You're going to feel stupid when the ulian wears off," one of the guards mutters as they wrestle the man into the cell.

"Ulian?" the man sounds hopeful and stops struggling. "Do you have some ulian?"

The other guard snorts. "No, we don't, and you don't need any more either."

"But we all need ulian," the man protests as the two guards drop him in an awkward heap on the cell bunk. "We're all going to live and die alone. I'll never see my mating marks on another's neck. I'll never hold my young in my arms. Ulian is the only solace."

The drunk's words make both guards stiffen, all good humor leeching out of their faces. "Shut up, Gilor. You don't know what you're talking about. There are Decanted women now. We're all going to find mates."

"Not enough," Gilor mumbles. "Not nearly enough of them. And why would they want us? We cage them. We make them into little pets." Gilor's voice takes on a sing-song quality. "Come here, little human. We'll feed you. We'll provide. But whatever you do, don't ask for freedom."

"Pienter shit," the other guard barks out, but Kilan can see real worry on both their faces. "You're just a gunner and drunk at that. You have no idea what you're talking about."

"My brother's Councilor Damir," he murmurs as he curls up on his side. "Council knows. Never going to find enough for everyone." Before either of the guards can demand more answers, Gilor starts snoring.

"Could he be telling the truth?" one of the guards asks the other as they file out of the cell.

"Gilor's in here every other week because he drinks and picks fights, I wouldn't trust anything that comes out of his mouth even if he wasn't floating in an ulian haze," the other guard declares dismissively. The two men that replaced Janin and Somar don't even look up from the data pad they're viewing as the other men lock Gilor's cell and leave. Kilan gets the feeling there's no affection between those two sets of males.

Looking at the drunk gunner, Kilan thinks over the information he just learned. He hasn't given much thought to the fact that so far, they've only found a handful of Decanted women. Like the rest of Hissa, he just assumed it would be a matter of time before enough were found to allow for rebuilding the Hissa population.

But what if Gilor's correct? What if there just aren't that many Decanted women out there to find? The Decanted women aren't just about keeping the Hissa from dying out, they're also the hope that keeps each Hissa male functioning. Without that hope, there's little reason for any Hissa to work hard and obey the Council.

In the years following the Great Death, Hissa was busy rebuilding and defending itself from those who saw the decimated civilization ripe for takeover. After the warfare calmed down, most Hissa remained focused on rebuilding because the Council convinced everyone that their scientists would be able to grow women to replace their lost loved ones. When that failed, the Council promised the population that the Bicoma would have the answers they needed.

What would the Council have done if Mara and Mian hadn't shown up with mating marks? Those two women were the first to reveal the compatibility of Decanted human women with Hissa men and opened up the real and tangible goal of finding as many Decanted women as possible.

Was faith in the Council already starting to wane when the

Decanted women were discovered? Could the trend of unquestioning loyalty to the Council be at an end?

With a sigh at such heavy thoughts, Kilan flops back down on his bunk and closes his eyes. In the end, it doesn't matter. Even if they can't find enough Decanted females he doesn't care because, for him, Deena's the only Decanted female he wants to worry about.

CHAPTER

22

Knowing that he should sleep and being able to are two very different things. Even though it's the middle of the ship's rest period when most are asleep and the lights in the brig are low, he's still wide awake. Gilor is fast asleep and snoring loud enough to echo in the room. The guards on duty are busy cleaning spare weapons and chatting about the latest armor modifications.

Giving up on sleep, Kilan sits up and leans his back against the bulkhead. His eyes feel gritty, and he's got a headache from tension and lack of sleep. Closing his eyes, he lets his head fall back against the cold metal wall behind him and pictures Deena. His favorite memory is when they were traveling to Gleem. There was a gas giant on the way and Deena circled it a few times, dipping into the upper atmosphere. As she skimmed around the planet, she created a pattern and did a few image captures as they got farther away.

Her utter delight and enjoyment made his heart swell, and after that, he located every gas giant in their path and let her play. By the time they got to Halm, the data banks in the main computer were full of captures of gas giants she played on. It was such a simple thing, flying around a gas giant and dipping in and out of its atmosphere, and yet it's so important to Deena. Not just something she enjoys, but evidence of her freedom.

Overwhelmed by his failure, he bangs his head a few times on the wall, cursing himself for not checking the biosystems.

"If you need your head caved it, I can do it for you," one of the guards offers, and the other snickers. Kilan doesn't bother responding. He's tempted to taunt the guards into opening his cell. But getting into a fight isn't going to help him or Deena, even if it might release some of the tension gathered in his gut.

Sounds of people in the hall draw all their attention, except Gilor, who's snoring never abates. Kilan strains his ears because something sounds familiar.

Deena.

One of the sounds coming from the hall is Deena's voice, and it's high-pitched and frantic. His heart starts to pound as the brig doors open up and half a dozen guards troop in, surrounding Telin, one of Deena's caregivers. He's cradling her in his arms, and she's pushing against him, wailing and crying at the top of her lungs.

When she spots him, she starts flailing wildly, and Telin is forced to stop and let her down or risk her hurting herself. The moment her feet hit the ground, she runs to him, ignoring Telin's shout to stop. Uncaring of the armor on their bodies, she starts hitting the guards who close ranks around her and create a wall between the two of them.

Her sobs are so violent her shoulders are shaking. "Please," she begs in a hoarse voice. "Let me touch him. Just let me touch him!"

Telin looks over to the brig guards who are standing at attention in the middle of the room. "Don't open his cell and be prepared to shock him to the ground if I order it."

"With pleasure," one of the guards says and picks up a shock stick.

"Telin!" Deena screams out desperately.

"Let her by," Telin orders in a tired, resigned voice.

The men part and Deena hurls herself at the bars of his cell. Kilan is already there, reaching between the bars and doing his best to hold her trembling, weeping form.

"Shhh," he whispers, kissing her forehead through the bars. "You're going to make yourself sick if you keep going on like this."

"Shut up," she whispers back, and he pulls his head far enough away to see her grinning face. Her eyes are red and swollen and her skin is too pale, but the smirk tells him the weeping and wailing is an act. Or at least mostly an act.

Ducking his head so the others can't see his relief or grin, he rubs one hand over her back and places the other squarely on her ass. She gives a little squeak when he squeezes, but then he feels her clever little fingers dipping into his pants.

It's not going to do his reputation any good if those in the room think he's aroused by the sight of his distressed mate. "Behave," he hisses when her hand finds his already stiffening cock.

"Someone's happy to see me," she murmurs back smugly.

"We're both always happy to see you," Kilan mutters. "But my current guards might beat me to death if they think I want to be intimate with you while you're bawling like a youngling having a temper tantrum." She gives him a squeeze that almost sends him to his knees before withdrawing.

"Just wait until I get you alone," she warns. "I'll show you a temper tantrum." He doesn't mention that the chance they will ever be alone together again is a slim one.

Grumbling from the others in the room draws his attention up briefly. All the faces regarding the two of them are frowning with a combination of disapproval and envy. Kilan just keeps himself from grinning at them because he's the only one that knows his clever Deena just tricked all of them.

"Who's your friend?" Deena asks, slipping her eyes over to indicate Gilor. "He's loud enough to wake the dead."

"Just another lost soul," Kilan says, making Deena sigh.

"Aren't we all?"

"My soul isn't lost," he tells her. "It's yours now."

"Is there a return policy?"

"Impudent human," Kilan murmurs, just managing to keep from barking out a laugh. Pressing his face against the bars, he captures her lips in another kiss, both grateful and disappointed when her hands remain chastely on his hips.

"Now that you've seen that he's alive and well, you will sleep," Telin says. "That's the bargain you agreed to."

Kilan watches Deena's face transform from a sly smile to distressed in the blink of an eye. She turns wide tear-filled eyes on Telin as her lower lip quivers. "Just a little longer," she begs. "Don't make me leave yet. I need more time."

Telin's face twists with frustration. "You're not supposed to be here at all," he explains patiently, and Kilan gets the feeling this isn't the first time he's said those words. "Velom was very clear. It's not good for you to be around this male. The sooner you choose another, the faster your health will improve."

"I did choose," she declares stubbornly, and Kilan watches her fight to keep her shoulder slump and her attitude docile. There's no doubt in his mind that if she could get ahold of a plasma rifle, she'd start shooting everyone in the room and attempt to fight her way to a shuttle. They might think she's a small, weak, human female, but Kilan knows that steel makes up her backbone.

With a long-suffering sigh, Telin shakes his head. "Come away from him, Mater Deena Clanless," he orders. "Remember our bargain and say goodbye."

Deena turns back to him, and he sees real fear in her eyes. "Bargain?"

"If they take me to see you, I calm down. If I don't leave when they tell me to, they're going to restrain me to the bed," she admits in a low, distressed voice. "I never thought this would happen to me," she continues. "I never thought I'd have to worry about being put in restraints." When he growls, she tries to give him a reassuring smile. "Hey, it could be worse."

"I failed you," he mutters, finally giving voice to the thought that's been plaguing him since they threw him in this cell.

"You couldn't have known what a sneaky bastard Mavito is," Deena says, casually dismissing his admission of guilt. "Besides, I knew we were on borrowed time. There aren't that many med suites that could handle a pregnant human. When I needed to give birth, they would've caught us."

"I didn't think of that," Kilan concedes, feeling more defeated than ever. "We were always doomed to be captured."

"We aren't alone," she reassures him. "All the other Decanted women are in our corner. I've already gotten dozens of messages from them and others who are busy petitioning the Council. It might take some time, but I think they'll eventually see reason."

Huffing out a humorless laugh, Kilan steals a last kiss. He can see Telin moving forward to drag Deena away from him.

"Eventually might be a very long time."

Just before Deena lets herself be drawn away, she shoves something small into his hand. "I'll make sure that eventually happens sooner rather than later," she promises as she lets Telin and the other guards draw her away. He watches with hungry eyes as she moves slowly, her smaller figure barely visible surrounded by her much larger escorts.

Once they're gone, he makes a production of slumping down on his bunk and looking defeated and forlorn. When he doesn't respond to their taunts, the guards go back to servicing their weapons and he feels safe enough to open his hand and see what Deena gave him.

It's a small gasket, old and worn. He'd been fussing with one of the modifications he'd made to the engine. She was sitting next to him chatting about her time with Lara and their old ship the Ally. When he handed her the old metal gasket, she wiggled in on her thumb and beamed at him.

"Oh, thank you, it's just lovely." Although her tone was mocking, she refused to take it off. She claimed it was something called a "wedding ring," a gift given between couples when they form the human equivalent of a Family Pact. She pointed to another one of her fingers and explained that they usually are put on that smaller digit, but since their union is unique, it's fine that it only fits on her thumb.

For some reason, he loved to see that battered gasket on her. It made him smile whenever she fiddled with it while she thought, rotating it with the fingers of her other hand. She did that so much that it started to gleam.

She never took it off. She worked, slept, bathed, and had sex with it securely on her thumb. Except now, it's no longer on her finger. He's holding it in his big hand instead.

He slides it on his smallest finger but finds it won't go past the middle joint. If he tries to wear it there it will fall off too easily. Looking around, his gaze falls on the bunk under him. He casually rips a piece of bedding and threads it through the ring, tying the ends together and then hanging it around his neck. Tucking it under his shirt, the warm metal comes to rest against his chest, making him feel closer to Deena somehow.

"I can do your mating mark tattoos, when you're ready," a voice says softly. Startled, Kilan looks up to find Gilor awake, but still lying curled up on his side. He doesn't sound drunk any longer and his eyes are sharp and focused. "My father was a marks tattooer, but there was no call for it when I was growing up, so he stopped practicing. I have his tools, and I know how to do it. It would be an honor to do yours."

"I would appreciate that," Kilan whispers, keeping one eye on the guards as he talks. Gilor appears to be a friend, and he doesn't want the man moved to a different cell because the guard decides Kilan doesn't deserve kindness.

"Soon then," Gilor states and closes his eyes again. Before Kilan can point out that he might spend the rest of his life in a cell, Gilor rolls over, and his snoring fills the room.

23

The ration pack tastes like spent casings from a biosystems filter, but Kilan forces himself to eat it anyway. Ration packs aren't particularly flavorful to begin with, but his separation from Deena is taking its toll and eating even a rare delicacy would be a chore at the moment. The only thing that keeps him chewing and swallowing is the fact that he needs to keep his strength on the off-chance Deena's able to fool her guards into letting her visit the brig again.

He just manages to get the last bite down his throat when he hears a muffled commotion in the hall. The guards from earlier are gone, replaced by two guards he's never met. Neither of the replacements seem particularly interested in engaging him in a conversation and refused him any requests for updates on Deena.

Another noise comes from the hall, but the door display doesn't chime and there's no verbal request for admittance. It's all very suspicious.

The two guards must have decided the same thing as well. As per training, the guards separate, one backing up to a defendable position in the far corner and the other engaging his

"Identify yourself," the forward guard orders. Both guards are so focused on the door that neither of them notices when Gilor slides from his bed. Kilan looks over and just manages to keep from making a sound of surprise when he sees the man is wearing a small breathing mask. He slips over to Kilan and hands him a second one, gesturing to put it on. Wordlessly, Kilan slides the mask over his nose and mouth.

The moment he's got the mask on, Gilor pulls a small cylinder out of his pocket and rolls it across the cell floor and out toward the middle of the brig. It pops open soundlessly, and although Kilan can't hear or see anything coming out of it, within moments, both guards drop unconscious to the floor.

Even the one with the helm up is knocked out. What was in that canister?

"They're down. Hold until I clear the gas!" Gilor yells as he crouches next to his cell door. A moment later, Kilan hears the distinct click of the cell door latch disengaging, and it swings open. Grinning, Gilor rushes forward and grabs the canister, slapping the ends closed. Then he goes to the brig control panel and turns the room vents on full for several minutes. He's holding some kind of small device in his hand, and when it beeps, he shuts down the venting.

"Clear!" he shouts as he takes off his mask and a dozen people file into the room.

They all busy themselves with tasks, but the only thing Kilan notices is Deena, who rushes toward him with a happy laugh. Pulling off his mask and tossing it aside, he hurries to the front of his cell.

"You're a sight for sore eyes," she says when she reaches his cell and slides her hands through the bars.

"What's going on?" Kilan asks, automatically pressing himself against the bars in an effort to get closer to her.

"Jailbreak," she explains succinctly. "Gilor over there masterminded it."

Kilan looks over to where Gilor is doing something on the room control panel, eyes narrowed in concentration. "Not so drunk," Kilan murmurs as he realizes the extent of the ruse.

"Don't gamble with that guy," Deena mutters. "He'll take you for everything. I lost ten credits to him before I figured out the bumbling drunk is all an act. And even after I figured it out, I still lost another two credits."

"Got it," Gilor calls out as he straightens up and steps

away from the panel. Kilan's door clicks open, and he steps out, sweeping Deena into his arms. "Why would they use a twenty-digit code for his cell door?" Gilor asks absently and stabs at the console a few more times. "Did they want him to die if there was an emergency and we had to get him out?"

"Probably," Kilan states, and Gilor winces.

"Sorry. I wasn't thinking," he admits.

"No point in pretending. A few of the guards would've been happy to flush me out an airlock."

"Bastards," Deena mumbles against this neck.

The two unconscious guards are dragged into one of the cells and efficiently stripped of not only their gear, but their clothing as well. Kilan eyes the pile of gear in the middle of the brig and looks over to Gilor. "One of the guards had his helm up. The gas shouldn't have affected him."

"His suit breather might have been tampered with by me," an unfamiliar face says with a cheerful grin. "I'm Armorer Minar."

Kilan eyes the many men around him, all wearing Steadfast uniforms. "All of you risk a great deal," he comments.

No longer smiling, Minar regards Kilan with a hard expression. "If we remain obedient, we risk more."

"We need to get moving," Laxon calls out from the hallway and Kilan looks over to find even more of the Steadfast crew standing out there with full armor and weapons held at the ready. This isn't just a jailbreak. This is a mutiny.

Minar gets his attention and gestures to armor on the floor. "Put that on."

Kilan complies as quickly as he can, even though the fit of the armor isn't quite right. He locks on the last piece, wincing a little when the edge of it digs into his arm. Hopefully, no one will look too closely.

"Helm up," Minar orders once Kilan finished with the last fastener. "You're going to take the right flanking position," he explains. "Mirror Somar. He'll be on the left. If we come across anyone, don't talk, and whatever you do, don't lower your helm."

Comprehension dawns on Kilan. He's just become a faceless guard in Deena's entourage. Simple and brilliant. "Observation cameras?" he asks.

"The cameras in here have been malfunctioning since yesterday," he explains with a glint in his eyes. "For the rest of the ship, I did the same thing you did. I set the program monitoring them to accept any activity as normal. The program will see Deena but won't raise any alarms, and no one will think to bring up any of the feeds if the alarms aren't triggered. That was a smart bit of thinking when you got her out the first time. Broken feeds would have drawn too much attention; unattended feeds don't look suspicious."

A massive male moves into the room from the hallway, and Kilan takes an involuntary step back. "Yopin?"

"Greetings, Pater Kilan," he says and looks over to the unconscious guards. "Serves you right," he mutters. "Sloppy."

"But you're one of Deena's guards. You were there when they separated us," Kilan sputters.

Yopin just gives Kilan a blank stare. "So?"

"He's the one who came to me," Gilor calls. "Helped get us all together and talking."

"And Gilor came up with the plan," Yopin says with a quick grin. "He's small with a quick wit."

"Everyone's small to you," Gilor mutters, then lowers his voice in an impersonation of Yopin. "Let me just pick up this shuttle and move it out of the way for you. There, now you can walk across the bay in a straight line. Is there anything else I can move for you, Pilot Deena Clanless?"

Most of the men chuckle at Gilor, but Deena's eyes are still on Yopin, who's grinning good-naturedly at the smaller Hissa.

"You started all this?" she asks Yopin.

Turning his gaze to her, the giant's expression softens. "I have to honor my mother."

"She's not your mother," Kilan mutters, confused, but Deena seems to understand.

"You're a good son," she murmurs. A little alarmed by this conversation, Kilan tugs Deena closer to him. Yopin notices and flashes him a quick grin. Then his face returns to the familiar stoic expression.

Men move around them, getting ready to leave. Gilor comes over and grabs his arm. "You promised I get to do your marks. We'll meet again, and I'll have my tools. I'll make it hurt as it should." With those words, he ducks back into his cell and latches the door behind him. With a last wink, he makes himself comfortable on the bunk.

"Our window is shrinking," Laxon calls from the hallway, his voice tense and tight. All the men around him move into position. Kilan engages his helm and takes up a flanking position as Deena walks unresisting into the center of the guards.

They move down the hall without trouble, making their way to the aft section of the ship that houses most of the cargo and landing bays.

"What's going on here?" a voice calls and the group halts. Kilan doesn't recognize the man, but the marking on his uniform indicates he works in navigation and logistics.

"Deena couldn't sleep," Yopin explains, stepping forward and lowering his helm. "She requested to walk the ship. Mender Dimon was consulted and said walking is the best exercise for a pregnant human." Out of all her guards, Yopin is the most unmistakable, and it won't occur to anyone to question him. His presence gives them legitimacy and means no one's likely to be suspicious of the group as a whole.

"Oh," the man says looking into the center of their group. "Pilot Deena Clanless," he breathes. He takes a step forward but stops when none of the guards surrounding Deena move out of the way to allow him to get any closer. Undaunted, he keeps talking. "It's an honor to meet you. I'm Assistant Navigator Hayon. If you'd like, I could give you a tour of the bridge or command room. We just expanded the telemetry system, and it's very impressive."

Moving forward just enough so she can be seen behind Yopin's large form, she gives Hayon a small smile. "Maybe another time," she tells him. "It took me forever to convince these guys to let me go for a walk, and they even promised me I could see some of the ships in the landing bays."

"Of course," Hayon says quickly and steps forward. "I have access to most of the ships because I'm on the Navigation and Components Maintenance crew. I can take you aboard any of the ships if you're interested. We don't have any Gerinas on board right now, but there's a beautiful Jeno in bay three."

If Kilan's attention wasn't so focused on Deena, he might have missed the microsecond of annoyance that flashes across her face. She's effectively trapped. Everyone aboard knows her passion for ships and flying, so although it isn't as sleek, an offer to get her hands on a Jeno would be hard for Deena to normally refuse. Especially considering Yopin told him they are just walking for exercise.

"Don't you have duties you should be attending to?" Yopin asks pointedly.

"I'm just finishing my shift," Hayon retorts. "And you must have read the order Mavito issued. If we can provide Deena with a pleasant distraction, we should make the offer. If you're walking her to the bays, there's no reason she shouldn't be allowed inside the ships. It's safe. She can't take off without the clearance codes, and the bays are shut down right now."

Deena glances over to Yopin, who remains silent, his expression stony. Kilan realizes it's going to be up to Deena to figure out how to extract them from the eager Hayon.

"I'd love to see the Jeno," she starts to say, but then her features twist in discomfort. "Oh no," she clutches her stomach dramatically and looks up to Yopin. "Where's the nearest elimination facility?"

All the men around her burst into movement. They rush her down the hall and shove her and Kilan into a tiny elimination room. Kilan disengages the helm as Deena makes a few retching sounds. Once she quiets, he pulls her into his arms, and they both listen closely at the door.

"Is she ill? I'll contact Medical!" Hayon's voice sounds panicked.

"Don't bother," Yopin tells him calmly. "The child makes her ill sometimes. She'll be fine once her stomach is empty."

"But medical should be here," Hayon insists.

"Sure, call them if you want to, but that'll annoy Mater Deena Clanless. She hates having to go to medical. Didn't you read the reports on Lara and Mian's pregnancies? This is a human thing, and it's normal."

"What a horrible evolutionary design," Hayon comments, his voice still distressed but less frantic. "Poor Mater Deena. Is there no relief?"

"She says the medication that stops it gives her a headache," Yopin comments casually. "She refused to talk to the guard who called medical last time she was ill like this. He was taken off her rotation." The implication is clear. Call medical and earn Deena's wrath.

"This is the first time I've ever heard him speak more than a few words," Kilan whispers to her as they listen to Yopin convince Hayon to abandon his idea of calling medical and return to his duties.

"He's just shy," Deena whispers back. "He's a chatterbox once you get to know him. But because he's so big and quiet, I think just about everyone just assumes he's antisocial." Then she gives a little snort. "It doesn't help that he carries around that blaster that's so heavy it's normally mounted on a walking unit. Who does that? I saw Telin try to pick it up to move it out of the way once. The guy almost fell over, and then Yopin walks up and just casually grabs it with one hand and sets it on the floor in the corner."

"Telin's not weak," Kilan mentions with wide eyes.

"No kidding," Deena retorts. "Yopin's just that strong. The guy's bigger than even Woken, and I thought he was as massive as you Hissa got. But turns out for all his intimidating size, Yopin's friendly and lonely."

Jealousy rears up in Kilan. "You're mine."

"No question about it," she agrees without hesitation. "Besides, I'm afraid of heights."

It takes Kilan a moment to figure out what she means, and then he's forced to stifle a bark of laugher.

"You can come out now," Yopin calls out, and Kilan engages the helm and opens the door. Most of the guards are facing away, anxious to meet any unexpected party before they spot Deena. "That was quick thinking," Yopin compliments her as they emerge.

"Would have been nice to tour the Jeno," Deena murmurs wistfully, and Yopin grins as they all resume their trek.

"The Jeno here isn't the only one in the universe," Yopin points out dryly.

"Yeah, but it's the only one I could steal and not feel guilty," she retorts and Kilan notices several of the guard's shoulders shaking. Deena's quick wit seems to be entertaining them as well. It strikes Kilan that she'd fit right in with the crew of the Steadfast. Willing to work hard, enchanted by the tech, thick-skinned enough to take the kind of verbal abuse that comes with serving in a military dominated by rough males, and caustic enough to give it right back to them.

And, of course, clever and charming enough to have every damn male eating out of the palm of her hand within moments of meeting her.

No, never mind. Her serving on a Hissa military ship is a horrible idea.

He puts himself just a little closer to her. He can't touch her. That would break the illusion of being a guard but being slightly closer than everyone else as they move down the corridor in tight formation helps ease his anxiety slightly. He can't wait to get her alone, to strip her down and cover her body with his own. To feel her soft skin against his again. They've only been apart for a few days, but it feels more like years.

They manage to make the journey without further incidents. Kilan isn't surprised to find another dozen males in the bay, rapidly prepping a ship. He almost laughs when he sees the ship and does laugh when he hears Deena's sound of disappointment.

"Why this one?" she asks, crestfallen. "If I had a grandmother, this thing couldn't outrun her. Even if she was missing a leg. Or even two legs. And maybe both eyes." Her words cause more laughter.

Before them is Deena's old ship Gradual, looking just as pathetic and patched together as it was for the brief time that he saw it before being rendered unconscious.

Chuckling, a man with engineer markings on his uniform walks up. "Don't look so disgruntled," he tells her. "The shell might be your old ship, but we gutted the rest of it. You have new Aghast engines, full Dimmerion control panels, a refurbished Rel navigation system, and we even managed to get a whole new biosystem installed."

"How?" Deena breathes out, her eyes sparkling with happiness.

"Mavito told us to dismantle it so you wouldn't be tempted to try and use it to escape," he admits. "It was set at a low priority, so we were only supposed to deal with it if we didn't have any other duties. When Gilor came to us, we organized off-duty personal to work on it. We got a lot of dirty looks because no one wanted us to take apart your ship, but that also meant no one was paying attention."

Tears gather in Deena's eyes, and Kilan watches as the man talking to her starts to panic. "I'm sorry! We just thought this was the best way for you two to stay hidden. Please don't be upset!"

Kilan lowers the helm and pulls Deena against him, giving the engineer a reassuring smile. "The child makes her emotional. If she could talk, I think she'd tell you she feels overwhelming happiness from everyone's kindness." Nodding emphatically, Deena points at Kilan with one hand and covers her eyes with the other, making suspicious sniffing noises.

The engineer looks relieved. He ushers them inside and quickly shows them all the modifications. Deena's quiet throughout but listens intensely and blinks furiously when the engineer is done.

"I can't thank all of you enough," she says in a voice thick with emotion. She's been nonchalant throughout the escape, even downright irreverent at times. Tears start sliding down her cheeks and Kilan realizes that she's not just moved by the gifts she's being given, but the fact that all these men are putting her freedom above everything, perhaps even their liberty.

"Are those bad tears?" the engineer asks carefully, and Deena snorts out a laugh.

"Anything but," she assures him. "Pick an adjective: excited, happy, jubilant, delighted." She takes a breath and reaches out to take his hand just as Yopin walks up. "But more than anything, they're grateful tears."

"Please stop that," Yopin begs.

Before anyone can say anything else, a klaxon sounds in the bay, and the men all charge into action. Yopin pushes a box into his hands. "Gilor told me to give this to you," and then he rushes to follow the engineer out the hatch. Deena moves to the pilot seat, getting there just before Kilan can usurp her position.

"You're emotionally compromised," he points out hopefully. "Perhaps I should fly right now."

She shoots him a look and smirks. "Suggest that again, and I'll make sure you're physically compromised."

"Fine," he grumbles as he drops into the co-pilot chair.

More klaxons start sounding, and Kilan casts Deena a meaningful look. Somehow, they've been discovered and the first hurdle they face is getting out of the landing bay before their path is blocked.

With an unrepentant grin, she starts the warm-up procedures for the ship's engines. That's when they both notice the landing bay blast doors starting to close.

CHAPTER 24

The invisible ion shield that keeps atmosphere in the bay but allows spacecraft to come and go at will, is slowly being replaced by the much more substantial blast doors, normally only closed when the Steadfast is engaged in battle. They're to keep enemy ships out, but they'll be just as effective at keeping Gradual in.

"Kilan!" Deena calls out as she pushes the ship to start moving, even though one of the engine indicators isn't reading ready yet.

"I see it," he responds stoically as he taps at the display in front of him. "Turning all maneuvering thrusters for forward flight," he reports. Because it's a dangerous thing to do, Kilan's forced to override several safety protocols to get all the nozzles pointed aft. They might burn some of the ship's fuselage, but they don't have a choice if they're going to try and beat the closing doors without main engines.

"I've got engine regulators on max warm-up," she tells him as she fires all the maneuvering thrusters. The ship starts moving awkwardly toward the bay opening. The massive hangar doors are already halfway closed. "I don't think we're going to make it."

As they watch, a figure moves at a startling fast clip toward the front of the hangar. It takes her a moment to figure out who it is because the helm on his armor is up, but once he runs by a standard size ambulatory stand it's obvious. Only Yopin is big enough to make one of those stands look small.

"What's he doing?" Kilan asks as the goliath sprints to the door, something long and heavy in his hands.

"I think he's—" Deena starts to say and then gives a little screech of surprise when the giant leaps at the last moment and lands hard right in front of the door's tracks, burying the long shaft tool he's holding into the lip of the door. A horrible grinding sound echoes through the bay, and the doors stop moving.

"He's saving our asses, that's what he's doing!" Deena announces as she looks down and sees that one of the engines has finally reached operational temperature. She smacks the control, and they shoot forward. Kilan almost tumbles out of his seat from the sudden movement but manages to grab the control console and stay in place. Pulling himself forward, he taps frantically at the panel.

"Lifting aft constraints from maneuvering thrusters," he tells her and seconds later, she feels the ship responding to her steering inputs. The change comes not a second too soon. Angling the ship slightly, she holds her breath as she fits them through the partially closed blast doors.

Metal sparks fly out as the ship brushes past.

"I hereby rename this ship the Near Miss," Deena announces with a whoop.

Kilan glances over at her jubilant pronouncement. "We aren't in the clear yet," he points out.

The display in front of them flashes with a comm link request. They both regard the request warily. "It could be Gilor or Laxon," he suggests

"Or Velom," she counters. "But yeah, we need to answer it."

Mavito's face appears on their display. "Cut engines and return to the Steadfast. Bay seven is open and available to land."

"Sorry about bay two," Deena calls out cheerfully. "Just send me the bill."

Mavito growls out a curse. "This is no time to joke."

"This is the perfect time to joke," Deena shoots back. "We're out of here. Do your worst, you one-eyed bastard," she challenges, and Mavito's surprised face is the last thing they see before Kilan cuts the link.

"One-eyed bastard?" he asks her with a wide grin. "Isn't that a slang term for . . ." He trails off with a pointed look down at his crotch.

She shrugs and blushes. "It's a dual-purpose insult." She looks down at the navigation display. "Looks like we've got company."

Several dozen ships are launching from the Steadfast and not just fighters. She can see there are several ships with the ability to latch on and forcefully board ships for takeover or rescue. She glances at Kilan. His expression isn't one to inspire confidence.

"We can't outrun them," he points out. "Not even with the new engines."

"We don't have guns, so we can't shoot at them either," she adds.

"And there's no convenient asteroid belt."

There don't seem to be many options. Both fall silent as another comm request flashes. They look at each other, and Deena shrugs. "Why not?"

This time it's Laxon's face that fills the screen. "Sorry for the delay," he says. "I'm sending coordinates. Plug them in and go for max burn."

"There's a lot of ships heading our way," Deena tells him. "I don't suppose you guys invented some new kind of Faster Than Light drive that works outside of gate range to get us out of here."

To her shock, Laxon chuckles. "Oh, don't worry about the little ships."

Looking over at the main console display, she sees that the Steadfast's fighters are almost on them. "They look pretty worrisome from here."

Kilan looks up from the navigation display. "Coordinates locked."

"Engaging full burn," Deena answers and feels the push of all three of the engines coming online. The telemetry and navigation computers start lighting up as the ship figures out where it is, and where it's going.

A fighter strafes them, flying close enough to set off all kinds of warnings on the control console. Kilan curses and Deena grabs the armrests of her chair and holds on with white knuckles. "And here I thought they wanted me alive," she mutters.

"They aren't firing at us," Kilan points out.

"They won't need to if they ram us," she gripes as another

fighter makes a pass so close, she swears she saw a face through a port window.

"Calm down," Laxon tells them.

"Easy for you to say," Deena retorts and then jumps when a specialty ship used for boarding vessels during war flies much too close. At least it didn't stop and latch on.

"They're scent mudding," Kilan shouts suddenly, startling Deena.

"What the hell is scent mudding?" Deena asks as yet another fighter gets too close for comfort.

"They're getting so close to us that the Steadfast's sensors can't pick up individual ships. The power signatures are all muddied together."

She sends him a perplexed look. "How is that going to help us? Once the Steadfast gets turned around, it'll catch up with us in no time."

"It's going to be hard to catch up to you," Laxon announces from the display with a jaunty chuckle that would do Gilor proud, "when the engines on the Steadfast seem to be failing. Shame that. Some engineer must have failed to do his job properly."

Switching the displays so they can view the Steadfast, both Deena and Kilan gawk. "Half the ship is dark," Kilan points out with a startled expression.

"They're using maneuvering engines only, none of the main engines are even firing," Deena says as she examines the image. "If I didn't know better, I'd assume the power relays got hit or something like that."

"Just keep the ship on course. Your escorts know what they're doing." With that, the link shuts down, and Laxon's gone.

"Do you think they're going to get in trouble for helping us?" Deena whispers.

"It's not 'if' they're going to get in trouble," Kilan answers grimly. "It's how much are they going to be punished."

Guilt crashes down on her. It must have shown on her face because before she can lament her role in the mutiny, Kilan grabs her hand and holds it tightly in his. "But the more important question you should ask is: would they do it all over again? And I know, without a doubt, the answer will be yes."

Leaning over in his seat, he captures her mouth with his. Despite their tense situation, despite the real chance that Mavito will manage to get his ship back online and catch up with them, she finds herself melting into the kiss.

Pulling away, Kilan cups her check in his hand and waits until she focuses her eyes on his. "Their answer and mine will always be yes. You are worth losing rank. You are worth being reprimanded. You are worth time in the brig. *You* are worth dying for."

Kilan pauses and takes a few ragged breaths. "You are worth living for too. You are worth risking everything, even my heart."

Throwing herself into his arms, she hugs him tightly. "You are worth loving," she whispers fiercely. "You're worth all the risks too."

They stay like that until the navigation system gets their attention. Returning to her seat, she finds that the coordinates put them right on the fringes of a merchant armada. Before either of them thinks to contact the armada lead ship, they're sent formation coordinates to follow. One of the rebelling Hissa must've already arranged for a spot for them in the Armada. Not only is the group massive, but at least a third of them are made up of the same make and model as theirs.

"They're heading to Havernook," Kilan reports and looks up to regard her with a quizzical expression. "There's nothing on Havernook."

"Yes, there is," Deena replies with a grin. "Havernook was terraformed last year. The place is the newest, hottest planet to buy space on. I did a couple of runs there. It's big, busy, and with two major cities that are already crowded. They even have a medium-sized space station and two moons full of domed cities. The traffic coming in and out is insane, and I think a second space station is being built to deal with it. It's probably going to become the biggest trading hub in this sector."

"The perfect place to get lost in the crowd," Kilan murmurs appreciatively.

"Your buddies are geniuses," Deena adds.

As they take their position in the merchant armada, their Steadfast escort breaks apart and heads in all different directions. Deena's sure they'll all return to the Steadfast, but by the time they weave their way through the most circuitous routes back, it will be impossible to backtrack them.

"We might still get caught," Kilan warns her. "The mutiny on the Steadfast won't keep other battleships from seeking us out."

Nonchalantly, Deena abandons the pilot's chair and crawls

back into his lap. "And there's a chance we'll get eaten by a mutated space bacterium. Or crushed by a rampaging Pienter. There's a lot of 'maybes' out there. The only thing I care about is the 'for sure' I've got right here."

With a chuckle, Kilan wraps his arms around her, careful not to squeeze her too tight and squish their daughter. "I think we should use that as a name," he comments. "For the ship."

"Ship designation For Sure," Deena laughs. "I like it. But which one of us gets to be captain?"

Kilan rubs her distended belly. "I believe she is," he murmurs as Deena feels her daughter do a backflip, landing with both feet directly on her bladder. Reluctantly, she wiggles off Kilan's lap.

"How about I meet you in the bunk? I'm just going to give our captain a tour of the elimination facilities first."

As she turns to close the door to the elimination room, she sees him hurry past, stripping out of his clothes. Her last image as the door shuts, is him naked and diving for the bunk.

CHAPTER

25

Gilor is even more of a genius than either of them originally realized. The box Yopin shoved into Kilan's hands is full of disposable credit chips, fake identification codes, and a small data pad of contacts that can be trusted to care for Deena when it's time for the actual birth to happen. As much as she appreciates the codes and the contact information, it's the credits that catch her attention.

"Where did all these credits come from?" she asks with wide eyes as she finishes tallying up the total. "There are just over twenty thousand credits here!"

"Gilor probably took up a collection among the crew," Kilan explains, unperturbed.

"Just took up a collection among the crew?" Deena squeaks. "I've never worked on a ship as big as the Steadfast, but even if I pooled the resources of the largest of my old crew, I'd maybe get up to thirty credits. Forty if I did well at a gaming night. Twenty thousand? This is inconceivable. Why the hell are they crewing on the Steadfast if these guys have that much wealth at their disposal to just give away?"

Kilan gives her a strange look, then draws her into a hug. "What else would they do? The credits we get from mining our moons means every Hissa is paid a very good wage. But there are no women or children. Who are we going to spend our credits on? What purpose do we have without a family to care for? The men work because it gives them a purpose when they have nothing else."

That shuts down Deena's questions right quick. "Yeah, right. I guess there's that," she mutters. "I've always known you guys are a rich species. I guess I just never really thought of it in terms of actual credits."

"There's always more credits to be made out there," he tells her. "Real wealth isn't in things that credits can buy. It's the woman who loves you and the child you help create. It's being able to protect your family and everyone else's. It's dying with the knowledge that you nurtured life and left behind a legacy of honor and love. Real riches come from those things. The credits just help us make it happen."

"Being able to buy something other than ration bars is nice too," Deena points out dryly. "In fact," she gestures over to the navigation system. "It looks like we're about to be able to spend some of those credits."

The navigation system is lighting up, telling them they've reached the area of space controlled by the Havernook space station. Kilan signals the station, and after being granted permission to approach, he requests docking arrangements. Deena holds her breath when he gives the station their new ship name and fake codes provided by Gilor. Her worry is unnecessary because the voice over the comm link gives them permission to dock, a berth number, and then sends basic information about the station's layout and laws.

"They don't have a glass dome here," Kilan murmurs as he maneuvers the ship into place so the automated docking controls can take over. "But they seem big enough to have some decent eating establishments. I never got to feed you on Halm. I'd like to today."

The trip with the Merchant armada took several weeks and, in that time, Deena and Kilan watched several different Hissa warships pass close by. None of them tried to intervene or even hail the armada with inquiries. Deena assumes it's because Gilor did such a great job hiding them that the Hissa commanders can't figure out which one they are among the thousands of ships in the armada. Or it might have something to do with the fact that every time a Hissa battleship gets too close to the armada, it seems to start having technical issues.

By the time they reach Havernook, Deena's starting to feel confident in Gilor and his mutiny to keep the Hissa fleet from being able to recapture them. Kilan must share her certainty, or he wouldn't be suggesting they walk on the station itself.

She gives him a big smile and rubs her distended stomach. "I'd love it if you bought me a meal. It seems our daughter is always hungry these days. And right now, she's craving some floranish."

Once the For Sure is docked and they arrange and pay for refueling, Kilan takes her hand and leads her to the main gallery. Just like on most stations, it's located near the bulk of the docks so potential customers don't need to go far to do their shopping. This time they're able to eat a meal without interruption, and Deena finds herself so greedy that she finishes her own and then eats half of Kilan's plate before she even realizes it. Laughing, he just orders himself a second plate of food and pushes the rest of his food over to her, so she doesn't need to reach so far over the table for it.

Red-faced with embarrassment but also smiling, she finishes off the plate of food just as his second plate arrives. He doesn't start eating right away. He eyes her silently until she cants her head. "What?"

"I'm waiting to make sure I won't be stabbed for my food if I turn my attention away from you," he says and then ducks away from her halfhearted punch.

"Eat your damn food," she growls out. She'll never say it out loud, but she loves this new version of Kilan. Ever since they joined the merchant armada, he's become lighthearted and easy with his affection. Although she saw hints of this Kilan before, after the mutiny, his former sullen and ill-humored attitude disappeared until only the happy and satisfied Kilan remained. Of course, he hasn't lost his quick wit or sharp tongue in the transformation.

After they eat, he insists they walk through some of the shops. He buys her bright-colored clothing in traditional Hissa styles. Deena lets him, only pointing out a few times that the delicate cloth and styles aren't very practical aboard the ship.

Secretly, she loves the clothes. The soft fabrics feel luxurious against her skin. And after so many years working in environments surrounded by utilitarian grays, the bright colors make her feel cheerful and buoyant. After feeding her, outfitting her in new clothes, and buying her a few trinkets, they wander back to the ship and argue amiably about where to go next.

That turns out to be the pattern they repeat on every station they visit, and it takes a little while for Deena to realize that Kilan's courting her. She wants to point out that it's a little late for courtship, that she's already his and their daughter is proof of that. But then she realizes Kilan needs this more than her. He needs to prove he can be a good mate when things are calm, not just when her life needs to be saved.

That realization makes her stop arguing with him when he buys her things, and she, in turn, praises him for every small thing he does for her. The month that follows is the best of Deena's life and an insight into what Kilan was like before Tarim's death. He can't seem to do enough things for her. If she didn't put her foot down, he might even carry her everywhere instead of letting her walk.

They're approaching Gleem station when Kilan broaches a subject that's been weighing heavily on her mind. "We need to think about where we'll go for our daughter's birth," he states, his body tense and his focus on the navigation display. Deena slumps back in her pilot chair and rests her hands on her swollen belly.

"I know," she sighs. "I've been thinking about it too. We can't go to the medical suite on Halm, like we originally planned. Even if the mutiny can keep the battleships away, that place just seems too vulnerable now."

"We have the list Gilor gave us," Kilan points out.

"And those stations seem too small. None of them have a lot of resources at their disposal," Deena sighs. "I'm not going to lie. I'm a little scared of the whole birth process. Maybe we should pay to have the baby extracted in a surgical pod."

"No surgical pod will be programmed to deal with human anatomy," Kilan argues.

"I know," she concedes. "I didn't think it was an option. I just thought I'd throw it out there." Although the discussion's been calm and considered, Kilan's face suddenly fills with fear.

"I can't lose you," he states, looking away.

Hurrying over to him, she wraps her arms around his waist and hugs him as tightly as her awkward body will allow. "You're not going to lose me," she tells him fiercely.

"You can't guarantee that," he whispers to her. "I could lose you. I could be forced to choose again, between suffering or death." She can tell she's lost him in his memories, so she rears back and slaps him hard across the face. That gets his attention and ire. Good, better he's annoyed than lost in past sorrow.

"Listen up," she says, her voice strong and confident because Kilan needs that from her right now. "I'm Deena Clanless. I'm the best pilot you've ever known and one hell of a survivor. I've never given up or given in. I fight for what I want and make no mistake, I want you. I want our daughter, and I want us all to grow old together. So, you better stay in the here and now, with me, or I'll hit you again and again because there's no way I'm leaving the best thing that's ever happened to me. Tarim might have been the love of your life, but she's gone and I'm here."

"It's you," he tells her in a hushed mumble.

"What?"

"I loved Tarim, but she wasn't the love of my life. You are," he states simply, and Deena feels the cursed tears start gathering in her eyes. "Her death destroyed me—but your death would end my life. Don't you understand? I breathe because you breathe. Without you, my body has no heart to pump blood."

Deena gives him a challenging look. "If I'm so important, then next chance we get, I want you to get the tattoos that all the mates get around their necks. The one that will match my mating marks." She watches as comprehension dawns on his face, then a myriad of emotions flow across his features. If Hissa could cry, she's pretty sure he'd be a sobbing mess.

"My heart," he chokes out. "I want that more than anything, but I was too afraid to ask."

Reaching out to touch the unmarked bare flesh at the base of his neck, she gives him a sassy grin. "I need to claim you properly before some other Decanted woman shows up and figures out how perfect you are."

"Not perfect," he argues as he sweeps her into his arms. "Just not broken anymore."

"To me, you're perfect," she murmurs to him. "And that's all that matters.

They stay like that until a request for a comm link flashes on their main display. They aren't close enough to any station for the station's computer to request control of their navigations for docking, so the request takes both of them by surprise.

"Probably just a request for code verification," Deena suggests. Kilan looks as apprehensive as she feels. Worry fills her chest, despite her assertion. Then she glances over at the navigation display, and her eyes get wide. "Pienter shit!"

CHAPTER 26

Kilan watches Deena's face drain of blood before he hears the telltale clicking coming from the display in front of her. Looking down at the display, he sees not only the Steadfast, but her sister ship, the Ardent. To his relief, no fighters have been deployed, but both of them are much too close for comfort. Much closer than any Hissa ship has gotten since the mutiny.

"What's happening?" Deena whispers and Kilan knows she's wondering the same things he is. Did the mutiny get put down? Are they no longer safe from capture?

"Perhaps they were able to bring the crew to heel because you're due to give birth soon," he guesses out loud. "Fear of losing you in childbirth might galvanize them into accepting Council dictates."

"We can't run," she states stoically as she glances over at the navigation display. "I'm registering a third Hissa ship at our stern."

"Let's finish the final approach to the station and dock," he suggests just as a request for a comm link blinks on the main console display again. Kilan looks over to Deena, silently asking her if they should answer it. Her face tense, she gives him one sharp nod.

"Open comm link request," he tells the computer, and three faces appear on their screen, Mavito, Gilor, and Laxon. Kilan expected to see Mavito or the Section Commander of the Ardent, not two of the men who led his jailbreak.

"We need to speak to you and Mater Deena," Mavito begins as Gilor waves cheerfully at them.

"Hello there! Up for a game of Noper or Renile?" Gilor asks, and Mavito shoots him a frustrated look.

"We talked about this, Gilor," he growls out. Gilor turns his attention to Mavito and just smirks. Deena leans over so they'll be able to see her face also.

"Don't make me tell Mater Deena not to talk to you. She trusts me," he taunts with a grin.

"I don't trust you," Deena interjects, her face softening into a smile. Kilan feels his shoulders relaxing slightly at Gilor's antics.

Gilor slaps his hand dramatically to his chest. "You wound me!"

"You won all my credits," she mutters.

"Technically, they were Velom's credits because you didn't have any," Gilor retorts. "So, I feel no guilt."

"Could we please focus on more important matters?" Laxon asks with a long-suffering sigh.

"The Council requests a meeting with you," Mavito announces.

Deena sneers at him. "They can request all they want."

Placing a calming hand on her shoulder, Kilan regards Mavito thoughtfully. "We won't return to Hissa for this meeting."

"Of course not," Laxon says. "The Resolute is here. Their communications array is powerful enough to reach Hissa if we clear the station's influence." Deena opens her mouth to protest, but Mavito holds up his hand before she can say anything.

"The Resolute will move into position and the Steadfast will act as a relay to you. You don't need to come aboard any of the ships. This isn't a trap," he assures them, but Kilan can tell Deena isn't ready to trust yet.

"That's why we're here," Gilor announces. "Laxon and I are proof that they're willing to listen to you. Yopin's here too if you want to talk to him." Deena nods and all three men move out of the way to allow Yopin's enormous chest to appear. They can just see the edge of his massive weapon as he leans over to put his head within the view screen's reach.

"Greetings, Mater Deena Clanless," he rumbles out. "I

miss you." Kilan leans over Deena, putting his face next to hers in a silent show of territoriality. Far from getting upset, Yopin's face brightens at the sight of Kilan. "Greetings Pater Kilan. It's good to see you and be able to use that title again. It's been too long." A cagey expression crosses Yopin's face. "We should practice sparring so you can be even more worthy of your mate."

Deena turns her face to put her mouth right next to his ear. "I might have told him how you managed to defeat a Regarian even after being shot," she whispers. He can feel the smile on her lips as she speaks. "He's a soldier. It impressed him."

Shuffling from the display brings both of their attention back. Yopin is scowling at someone off-screen. "Then move," he says. "I'm not handing you my weapon. If it's poking you, then re-position yourself."

Kilan muffles a laugh at the unflattering muttered response off-screen. Yopin ignores his upset crewmate.

"Is all of this true? Does the Council want to speak to us, not capture?" he asks once Yopin is focused back on the screen.

With a nod, Yopin smiles. "There were many orders to capture, but we all refused," he explains. "Most of us refused to hunt you down. Navigators couldn't pinpoint your locations. Ships kept having issues so they couldn't deploy from the bays. Communications were always breaking so we couldn't stay in contact with homeworld. They tried to put us in the brig, but the guards and soldiers refused. They wanted to take my weapon," he shows them a menacing grin. "But I dared them to try. There were too many of us who refused orders. Ships can't fly if everyone's in the brig."

A delighted laugh comes out of Deena, and Kilan finds himself grinning at Yopin. "You're an honorable male," he tells the giant soldier.

A hand appears in the picture and shoves ineffectually at Yopin. The giant slides a glance over and then reluctantly moves out of the viewscreen. Laxon moves back into view.

"Do you need to talk to anyone else? The flight crew, engineering crew, and everyone else that helped us that night we got you off the Steadfast are all here, ready to assure you the offer to talk with the Council is real and not just some ploy. We're all also ready to shut down every ship in the Hissa fleet if they do anything you don't agree to."

"Then we agree to talk," Deena says. "But only talk."

"Maintain your position in orbit around the station,"

Mavito commands as he pushes himself into the view screen. "When all the ships are in place, we will send a link request. Councilor Pavor will act as the voice and face of the Council, but all of them will be observing the meeting." His words feel like a warning so Kilan nods soberly.

"Understood," he says, then shuts down the link.

Before Deena can comment, he scoops her up and sits down in her chair, settling her in his lap. "It's too uncomfortable to lean over to see the display," he explains, making her grin. He runs his hands over her swollen belly and feels their daughter kick. Deena grunts from the movement.

"I think our daughter is eager to meet us," Kilan murmurs.

"I think our daughter and I are already arguing," she grouses.

The display flashes with a link request. They both watch it flash for a few moments. "Do it," she whispers, placing one hand in his and interlacing their fingers together.

"Open comm link request," he commands the console, and Counselor Pavor's face appears. Most of the Councilors are much older, showing their ages with lines on their faces and fading color in their scale patterns. But Pavor is far younger than the rest. Despite his youth, he tends to be the calmest and most levelheaded, even among the Council members who are generally picked for those exact traits. Kilan remembers Mavito joking with him once that if Pavor became any more sedate, he might be mistaken for being dead.

"Pilot and Mater Deena Clanless, Pilot Kilan, first male of the family Uman, we the Council greet you," Pavor intones formally.

"What do you want to talk to us about?" Deena asks, her tone of voice as brusque as her word choice. Kilan has to admit, he's not particularly interested in trading pleasantries either, not with their future at stake.

"I can see you'll be ready to bear your child soon," Pavor comments, glancing down. He can probably just see the top of Deena's belly in his view screen. "This is one of the reasons we are so eager to speak with you. It's our hope that you'll see your way to coming back to Hissa for the birth. No Menders or medical suites will be as well informed or capable as ours."

"I'm sure you've got the best of intentions," she answers. "But I'm going to decline."

"Before you refuse, let me tell you what's been

happening," Pavor says quickly, showing more animation than Kilan's ever seen from the placid councilor.

"What are you talking about?" Kilan asks. He expected promises of safety, or an attempt to trigger Deena's maternal instinct to seek out only the best for her child. Instead, Pavor wants to give them an update on current events?

"Over the last few months there's been social unrest," Pavor explains. "All of Hissa has been divided over the treatment of Deena Clanless. The other Decanted women have been very vocal about their opinions even before your escape from the Steadfast. Afterward, tensions only escalated."

"It's good to know someone's paying attention," Deena grumbles.

"This isn't just about you," Pavor tells her, and for the first time, his face registers an emotion: determination. "What we do with you will set a precedence for future Decanted women, especially those that come to us as free women, not ones we purchased as slaves and bring home to set free."

Deena doesn't look appeased at all. "It's not freedom if we don't have choices."

Pavor nods emphatically in agreement. "Freedom can't always be safe. And that's the crux of the division. Do we allow the Decanted women their freedom or do we keep them safe, even from themselves? The two options are often mutually exclusive."

"Hey," Deena protests. "It's not as if I was trying to stab myself with a knife or anything."

Pavor pins her with a knowing look. "Do we need to talk about the fatal situation the Hissa saved you and Lara from? Or the time you knowingly flew into a warzone by yourself?"

"Fine, throw a raider attack in my face," Deena sputters. "No one invites a raider attack, you know!"

Kilan notes that she deliberately doesn't comment after the second situation, probably because there's absolutely no logical defense and she knows it.

"It's true that you didn't seek to cause yourself harm," Pavor agrees. "But being out in the galaxy instead of securely ensconced planet side means a risk of attack, or engine malfunction, or any one of hundreds of things that can go wrong. I know you see it differently, but our intention was never to take away your independence. The focus was always your safety."

"Velom drugged me," she shoots back. "Repeatedly. They would hold me down and pull up my shirt to scan me. All. The.

Time. You let them do that to me. You let them make me into a type of slave. Nothing better than a broodmare. A walking, talking womb."

Her body is shaking from intense emotions, so Kilan puts his mouth close to her ear. "Easy, my love," he whispers. "Take a few deep breaths."

Pavor doesn't rise to the bait. He simply waits for her to refocus on him and then starts talking in his calm, patient voice.

"Imagine your daughter is about to board a ship and fly off on her own with no crew and no backup. How would you feel?" The question makes Deena tense, and Kilan feels Pavor's words like a punch to the gut. They remain silent as Pavor continues. "Would you request that she not go? Would you fight with her about her choices? Would you insist she hire a crew? Would you demand to go with her to help keep her safe? If she refused all these options, would you lock her away to keep her safe?"

With a ragged breath, Deena shakes her head and buries her face against Kilan's chest. He feels her hot tears soaking his shirt and looks up to Pavor. "That was unkind, Councilor Pavor."

To his credit, Pavor doesn't look the least bit triumphant. "Both of you need to understand the extent of the emotions being dealt with here. Half the miners on Diminish and almost all the miners on Brimming went on strike, demanding Deena be brought home. In response, the pilots refused to run supplies to either moon in support of Deena's freedom. That's just one example. I have dozens more I can share where our society is dividing and ripping itself apart because of one Decanted female."

"You said it yourself. It's not just about Deena," Kilan spits out. "Don't put the blame all on her."

"No, you're correct. That was unjust of me," Pavor backtracks quickly. "But right now, the entire focus is on Deena."

Keeping her head buried in his chest, Deena clutches Kilan's hand. "What should I do?" she asks, her voice sounding devastated.

"Before you answer, Kilan," Pavor says quickly. "Let me explain what the Council wishes to offer both of you." Deena lifts her face from Kilan's chest with a sniff.

"Go on," she says.

"We are trying to find a waypoint between assuring your safety and granting you freedom. If you return to Hissa to have the child and agree to only fly in Hissa-controlled space for the first few years of the child's life, we agree to allow you the same freedom of movement everyone else has."

"What if I get in my ship and start leaving Hissa space?" she asks suspiciously.

Pavor gives her a wide smile. He's been waiting for that question. "Then we will simply deploy a battleship to accompany you. If you decide to visit Gleem, it will be right behind you. If you decide to haul cargo, it will be your shadow. We'll never force you to stay or lock you in again, Mater Deena Clanless. But we'll do everything in our power to keep danger from taking you away from us."

"You'd send an entire battleship to keep me company, even if all I'm doing is hauling freight?" she asks incredulously.

"My heart, why is that so unbelievable?" Kilan asks with a small frown. He gestures to the navigation display that shows the Steadfast's position: they're maintaining a steady distance to their port side. Her face colors.

"Right," she huffs out. "But I always think of those guys out doing their duties and running into us, not that they're deliberately following us."

Now it's Kilan's turn to look incredulous. "We've seen Hissa battleships at every station we've visited since we left the Steadfast. How could you think that was anything but them watching over us?"

She shoots him one of her adorable smirks. "Blatant disregard for the mountain of evidence right in front of me? Willful ignorance? Deliberate denial? I use the same mental gymnastics to pretend you're cute, so I'd just go with it if I were you." Kilan gives her a little pinch, and she giggles through her tears as she slaps his hand away.

"It'll be very similar to what we're doing now," Pavor agrees. "But instead of non-destructive crew sabotage keeping you from being captured, a policy of 'guard but don't impede' will prevail."

"Can I just hang out on Steadfast?" Deena asks hopefully. "That ship travels the farthest out of all your battleships. Can I just travel with them? I could pilot the drones or do restocking to different stations."

"Eventually, if you want to. Or you could join on with the Abundant. It's one of our merchant ships, and I think you might enjoy it more than a battleship. But for right now, we need your presence here. Our society is being torn apart from the inside, and we need you to be seen smiling, laughing, and content to be on

Hissa with Kilan so the division can be healed."

"Let me talk to Kilan," she says and taps the display to mute it, then pushes at the control console to swing their chair around and give the view screen their back. Kilan lifts his feet so the chair can swing freely and once they're facing away, waits for her to speak first. He always does this now, waits for her input before saying anything. It's one of the many things he does to show her that he's willing to follow her, not dictate to her.

"Can we trust them?" she asks Kilan, looking to him with tired eyes.

"We can," Kilan assures her, cupping her cheek in his free hand. "Do you wish to rest for a while? We could go back to Hissa. You could have the baby, and we could both teach at the flying school until we feel like doing something different."

"As long as I don't have to do any flights to the moons and back," she murmurs, resting her head against his chest. He wraps his arm around her. "I have to admit, it'll be nice to settle planet side for a little while."

"There's no shame in wanting to walk on dirt instead of deck plates," he murmurs to her, and she laughs.

"I didn't say anything about dirt," she shoots back. "I was thinking I want to buy a glider of my own. Your homeworld has some great skies for gliding."

"Your homeworld too, Deena," he reminds her. "You're not Clanless anymore."

"What?"

"It's your homeworld too. They're your people. They love you so much that half of them demanded your freedom and the other half demanded your safety, but all of them demanded these things because they love you. You're adored, my heart. Whether you want to be or not. You might have chosen the name Clanless, but it's no longer applicable. You have an entire civilization as your family now."

Huffing out a laugh she looks up at him, tears swimming in her eyes. "I want to go home," she whispers. "I've always wanted to go home. I just didn't know where it was."

He gives her a gentle kiss just as a few ever-present tears escape her eyes. "Let me show you the way."

CHAPTER

27

Panting, Deena reaches out to grab Mender Dimon, but he's too fast for her, and she ends up grasping empty air. She has a feeling this isn't the first time he's had to move quickly to avoid injury from a birthing human woman.

"I warned you this might happen," he reminds her gently. Kilan grabs her clawing hand and brings it to his chest, not even wincing when she digs her nails into him.

"This hurts!" she yells. "You said when I told you it hurt, you could make it stop hurting!"

"Not if you waited too long," the Mender says for the third time. "Your daughter is almost here. You need to bear this pain just a little longer."

"Let me rip your nut sac out through your mouth and see how you bear the pain," she mutters and hears Mara laugh. "It's going to get worse before it gets better," she assures Deena cheerfully.

"Shut up, bitch," Deena grouses, making both Mara and Lara laugh.

The medical display on the wall next to her makes a few sounds, and Mender Dimon murmurs something she doesn't hear.

Kilan leans over and places his head near hers. "If I could take the pain for you, I would." The mating marks tattooed on his neck are proudly displayed by his low-collared shirt. As the pain of the contraction eases, she reaches up a hand to run her fingers over the pattern.

"I love you so much," she whispers to him.

"You're my heart and soul," he whispers back. They stay like that until the next contraction makes her sit up and scream with pain as she works to bring her daughter into the world. Kilan never lets go of her hand, never stops whispering to her, and when their daughter slides into Mender Dimon's competent hands, both sigh with relief.

"Deena and Kilan, of the family Kin, may I present to you, your daughter," Mender Dimon says as he hands the bloody and screaming infant to Kilan. Leaning over, Kilan cradles the newborn between them.

"I know what I want to name her," Deena says as she stares in awe at the little person she created. Everyone crowds around to get a look at the latest addition to the Hissa civilization.

"I told you any name you want I'll agree to," Kilan assures her.

"Welcome to the family, Tarim, first daughter of the family Kin," Deena announces, and Kilan meets her eyes. Deena hears some sniffing from others in the room but ignores it. Her entire focus is on Kilan.

"Do you mean that?" he whispers.

"With all my heart," she says.

"I don't deserve you," he murmurs. "I never thought my life would be this perfect."

"Don't worry. It won't be for long," she gives him a cheeky grin as their daughter continues to scream inconsolably. "I already bought her a miniature glider to practice in."

Kilan frowns as Deena starts laughing, pulling her daughter to her breast. "You don't know it yet," she whispers to her daughter as the baby finds a nipple and stops crying in favor of food. "But you're the luckiest girl."

She glances up to Kilan whose face shows nothing but love and amazement as he watches their daughter nurse. "Very lucky, just like your mama."

Dear Readers,

Thank you for reading *Defying Kilan*. If you want more Hissa Warrior the next book, *Healing Mavito*, is available. The moment Mavito was sweet and protective of Deena I knew I wanted to tell his story. He and Raleen are perfect for each other!

I hope you enjoyed *Defying Kilan* enough to leave a review! As an indie writer without the support of a publishing company, I need all the help I can get. Your good reviews keep me writing.

You can find links to my social media and free novellas on my website: www.rk-munin.com

Cheers,
Rye

OTHER BOOKS BY RK MUNIN

-Science Fiction-

Hissa Warrior Series
Rescuing Halin (Mian and Halin)
Buying Tiran (Mara and Tiran)
Tempting Selon (Lara and Selon)
Defying Kilan (Deena and Kilan)
Healing Mavito (Raleen and Mavito)
Claiming Yopin (Mouse and Yopin)
Teasing Woken (Safena and Woken)
Defending Revin (Kamaril and Revin) – Coming soon

Human Pets of Talin Series
Loving Captivity (Sora and Searin)
Escaping Captivity (Lakin and Dalt)
Negotiating Captivity (Nalia and Derani)
Fighting Captivity (Zia and Palforma)
Tender Captivity (Jinna and Holian - This is a novella you
can get for free by signing up for my newsletter)
Craving Captivity (Lasha and Tamerin)
The Twelve Nights of Halloheen: A holiday mashup novella
(Isla and Tisuran)
Stealing Captivity – Coming soon

Origins (A Human Pets of Talin Series)
Creating Captivity (Ari and Bazium)
Gossamer Chains (Rain and Hesarium)
Golden Cages – Coming soon

-Paranormal /Urban Fantasy-

Ours Evermore Series
Two Wolves for Soren (Soren, Kalli, and Quinn)
A Hacker, Vampire, and Chimera Walk into a Bar….(Tobias,
Briar, and Memphis)
When Darkness Meets Dawn (Imani, Lex, and Mac)

Tag, You're It (Short Story)
Kidnapping Their Third (Cora, Pike, and Kimble) – Coming
soon
Pastries on a Plate and Blood in a Mug (Novella) – Coming
soon

Alpha Series
Alpha Mage (Emma and Kade)
His Alpha Mage (Avery and Jason – Novella)
Alpha King (Cathleen and Lazlo)

New Clan Series
Stray Wolf (Steph and Eli)
Lost Lion (Maeve and Cyrus)
Reluctant Cervid (Tavi and Donovan)
Broken Thorn (Sabina and Theodosius)